"How can we be sure we make the right decision, Eric?"

His eyes took on that warm, crinkly look Bree loved. "Prayer helps. We trust God to bring us the right parents for Charity. And we trust Him to give us the wisdom to recognize them when we meet them."

"You make it sound so easy." Bree shifted in her chair. What she wanted to say was, *When the time comes, how do I let Charity go?*

"A penny for your thoughts," mused Eric.

The heat rose in Bree's cheeks. "It's nothing. I was just thinking of Charity and how much I want the best for her."

"So do I," said Eric with a surprising little rumble of emotion in his voice.

CAROLE GIFT PAGE

writes from the heart about issues facing women today. A prolific author of over 40 books and 800 stories and articles, she has published both fiction and nonfiction with a dozen major Christian publishers, including Thomas Nelson, Moody Press, Crossway Books, Bethany House, Tyndale House and Harvest House. An award-winning novelist, Carole has received the C.S. Lewis Honor Book Award and been a finalist several times for the prestigious Gold Medallion Award and the Campus Life Book of the Year Award.

A frequent speaker at churches, conferences, conventions, schools and retreats around the country, Carole shares her testimony (based on her inspiring new book, *Becoming a Woman of Passion)* and encourages women everywhere to discover and share their deepest passions, to keep passion alive on the home front and to unleash their passion for Christ.

Born and raised in Jackson, Michigan, Carole taught creative writing at Biola University in La Mirada, California, and serves on the advisory board of the American Christian Writers. She and her husband, Bill, live in Southern California and have three children (besides Misty in heaven) and three beautiful grandchildren.

A Child Shall Lead Them
Carole Gift Page

♥ *Love Inspired*®

Published by Steeple Hill Books™

STEEPLE HILL BOOKS

Steeple
Hill™

ISBN 0-373-87157-0

A CHILD SHALL LEAD THEM

Visit us at www.steeplehill.com

Printed in U.S.A.

The Lord your God in your midst,
The Mighty One, will save;
He will rejoice over you with gladness,
He will quiet you in His love,
He will rejoice over you with singing.
—*Zephaniah* 3:17

To my dear sister, Susan Gift Porter.
Susi, you are awesome! So talented, so caring,
so committed to our Lord. I love you with
all my heart, and I'm so proud of you.
You are my soul mate, my friend, my partner in
prayer. You bring joy to so many, especially when
you step out on stage and sing so vibrantly of your
Redeemer. Thank you for your constant love,
encouragement and support!

Chapter One

Brianna stood in the doorway of the music room in an oversize *V*-neck T-shirt and stone-washed jeans, her tawny hair framing her luminous face, her large, velvet green eyes looking worried. "Daddy, are you coming downstairs to dinner?"

She had assumed a tentative stance, her head cocked just so, one hand on the doorjamb, her rosy lips pursed questioningly.

Andrew's heart lurched. Something in his daughter's winsome face reminded him of his beloved Mandy. Like mother, like daughter. He half expected to see Brianna cradling one of her scraggly strays in her arms—a mongrel pup, a scrawny alley cat, a wounded bird. Since she was three she had managed to drag home every lost and homeless animal within a ten-mile radius of La Jolla. Mandy had been the same way, nurturing and comforting every ragamuffin child, every downtrodden soul, every wounded spirit. It was what had made her a great minister's wife.

"Daddy? Did you hear me? You look a thousand miles away."

Andrew's reverie broke. "I'm sorry. What did you say?"

"I said dinner's ready. It's Friday, so Frannie made her usual spaghetti. Your favorite."

"Sounds great, sweetheart." Frannie, his youngest, had designated herself chief cook and bottle washer after Mandy's death six years ago. In fact, all three of his daughters had appointed themselves their father's keepers, mollycoddling him like doting little mothers. His three precious girls: Cassandra, Brianna and Frannie. What would he have done without them?

But now there were just two left at home.

He cleared his throat and said with more enthusiasm than he felt, "Tell Frannie I'll be down in a minute, okay?"

Brianna lingered in the doorway, looking unconvinced. Yes, no doubt about it. His middle daughter, with her wholesome peaches-and-cream, girl-next-door attractiveness, was at heart a mother hen—a cross between Mother Teresa and Florence Nightingale. And now Andrew was the object of her overweening concern.

"You're thinking about Cassie, aren't you, Daddy."

Andrew swiveled on the mahogany bench, his right hand remaining on the shiny black grand piano. Cassie's piano. "You caught me, baby cakes," he confessed. "I guess I've been thinking a lot about Cassie this week."

"Oh, Daddy." Brianna crossed her arms and rocked on one heel. "Cassie's on her honeymoon. She and Antonio are so happy. I've never seen two people so in love...except you and Mom."

"And I'm happy for her," Andrew said quickly.

"It's just…well, this old house hasn't seemed so empty since…"

"Since Mom died," said Bree softly.

Andrew nodded, a painful knot in his throat. He looked away before his daughter read too much in his expression.

Too late. Her eyes brimming with sympathy, Brianna crossed the room and twined her slender arms around her father's neck. In Andrew's memory flashed the image of a jubilant child, running, skating, dancing, her hair flying in the wind. "It's okay to feel sad sometimes, Daddy," she whispered. "I miss Mom, too."

Andrew ruffled his daughter's silky hair. "I'm fine, doll baby. You go downstairs and tell your sister to get out the king-size bibs because I'm ready to eat spaghetti!"

"She already has them out, Daddy. One for each of us, like always." Brianna drifted back to the doorway and fluttered her fingers in a wave. "Don't be long, or the pasta will be cold."

"One minute. I promise."

After Bree had gone, Andrew inhaled sharply and turned his gaze to the family portrait on the piano, taken the year before Mandy learned she had cancer. They were at the beach, having a picnic, building sand castles, collecting seashells, frolicking like children. Looking like windblown, ragtag beach bums.

When a stranger offered to snap their picture, they laughed uproariously. Why not? It would be a silly, hilarious memento for posterity. So Andrew, his wife and daughters all stood arm-in-arm like disheveled comrades, smiling, on the verge of side-splitting laughter on that dappled, sun-washed beach. They had been oblivious to the horror lurking in the shadows, nipping at their heels.

For Andrew, those dark, devastating days seemed like another lifetime now...watching his beloved Mandy succumb moment by moment, inch by inch to that ravaging monster called cancer. Only his faith in God and his darling daughters had kept him sane. After Mandy's death, his girls had rallied around him and gradually turned their grief-stricken house into a rollicking, joyous, fun-filled homestead again.

But as devoted as his lovely daughters were to him, over the years Andrew had grown increasingly concerned about them. It wasn't right for three grown, vibrant young women to remain in their father's house, putting their own lives on hold for his sake. Sure, each daughter had a fulfilling career, but they needed to be out dating, making the acquaintance of suitable young men. They needed to be setting wedding dates and getting married and bringing home precious grandbabies that he could spoil the way he had spoiled them.

That's why, almost a year ago now, he had resolved to help things along, to give his girls a proper nudge in the matrimonial department. And, thank God, it had worked for his oldest daughter, Cassandra. Just last Saturday, hadn't he himself, the proud papa, officiated at the most gorgeous wedding on earth? Hadn't he choked with love and pride as his darling Cassie said her vows and became the radiant bride of the dashing Antonio Pagliarulo? Hadn't he smiled with satisfaction and, yes, relief as Antonio whisked Cassie off to a Mediterranean honeymoon?

One down, two to go, as the saying went. Now he just had to find husbands for his two younger girls, Brianna and Frannie. And that would not be an easy feat, for both girls were too devoted to their careers even to give a man a passing glance—Bree with her work at the family counseling center and Frannie with her sculpting and painting. Both girls were entirely too entrenched at home, fussing like nursemaids over their widowed father, to realize that the world contained a vast array of eligible bachelors.

Even now, as Andrew sat in the music room and studied the family portrait atop the grand piano, he knew his concerns were legitimate. If he let them, his remaining daughters would stay at home forever—at least until he went to be with his precious Mandy, or, heaven forbid, he took another wife.

He almost had. Taken another wife, that is. While Antonio was courting his sweet Cassie, Andrew had found himself enraptured with Antonio's widowed mother—the audacious, unpredictable Juliana Pagliarulo. Her exotic beauty had tantalized him just as her flamboyant personality had captivated him. And, amazingly, she had seemed equally enamored with him.

But, of course, the timing wasn't right for a serious romance. These days Juliana had her hands full helping her disabled daughter learn to walk again. And a fine job she was doing. Belina, a lovely, blossoming young woman, was well on the road to recovery. At Cassie's wedding she had served as a bridesmaid, walking proudly, victoriously down the aisle on canes. There wasn't a dry eye in the house. In fact, Belina nearly stole the show from Antonio and Cassie, and no one could have been happier about it than they.

But it wasn't just Juliana's parental responsibilities that had nipped their romance in the bud. If Andrew was honest with himself, he was equally to blame. As much as he cared for Juliana, he still couldn't quite relinquish his emotional hold on Mandy. He knew he was being foolish, holding on so desperately to his memories, finding his solace in a woman who had been dead for six long years.

A few times his daughters had caught him speaking aloud to Mandy, as if she were still alive, still in the room with him, listening to him unburden his heart. But his daughters' concerned glances weren't warranted. As eccentric as he might be, he wasn't addled enough to believe Mandy could actually hear him (although wasn't it possible she was listening from heaven's portal?). The problem was that he had become so accustomed over the years to Mandy's presence, her patient smile, her gentle voice, her listening ear. She was a hard habit to break. But, in spite of his grief, he wouldn't wish Mandy back with him. Far better that she was with the Lord, free of pain and basking in His love.

Andrew heard a scratch at the door and turned just in time to glimpse his mongrel, mop-haired dog push the door open and bound inside. Ruggs half scrambled, half slid across the polished hardwood floor, his shaggy, hirsute form landing in a disheveled heap beside the piano bench. Andrew reached down and massaged the panting animal's floppy ears. Ruggs rewarded him with a lick of his rough, wet tongue on Andrew's chin.

"Well, Ruggsy boy, it looks like my daughters called in the troops...or should I say, one furry, four-footed storm trooper. "You go back downstairs and tell my girls I'm on my way." He chuckled as Ruggs yipped eagerly. "Okay, boy, bark if you have to. They'll get the message."

Andrew followed the big, lumbering dog downstairs. Ruggs was one of Brianna's foundlings—a neighborhood stray she had rescued nearly ten years ago from the clutches of an overzealous dog catcher. Bree had promised to find the starving pup a good home; the home turned out to be Andrew's. Now Ruggs was as much a part of the family as anyone. The girls adored the ungainly pooch and forgave his every vice, including chewing Andrew's leather shoes to shreds and pilfering steaks from the backyard grill.

With much howling, Ruggs announced Andrew's presence in the dining room. Andrew took his place at the head of the table, flashing an apologetic smile at his two daughters. "Hope I'm not too late," he said as he fastened Bree's hand-stitched, terry-cloth bib around his neck. Bree had made him the enormous bib several years ago as a practical joke. Andrew was known far and wide for his clumsiness; he could never maneuver his way through a spaghetti dinner without strategically positioning a dollop of tomato sauce on his best dress shirt. So the bib was a welcome defense against all the loose spaghetti strands that threatened to attack.

Oddly, the bib idea caught on, and soon everyone in the family wanted one. Then guests who came to dinner began to expect them, too, so Bree gladly stitched a stack of them, customizing each one. The bibs became wonderful conversation pieces, always good for a laugh.

And a laugh is just what we need these days, Andrew mused to himself as he smoothed his bib over his starched white shirt. "Looks good," he told Frannie as she set heaping bowls of pasta and spaghetti sauce on the linen-draped table beside a tossed salad and a platter of garlic cheese toast.

"Your favorites, Daddy," she said, sitting down.

"You bet." He reached for his daughters' hands, bowed his head, and asked God's blessing on the food, adding softly, *"Lord, take special care of Cassie and*

*Antonio, wherever they are tonight. Give them a won-
derful life together. And fill this empty house with lots
of life and laughter again.''*

As they ate, Brianna gave Andrew several curious
glances, as if she had something to say but didn't know
quite how to say it.

"What is it, Bree?" Andrew prompted. "Got something on your mind?"

Bree twirled a spaghetti strand on her fork. "I was
just thinking, Daddy..."

"Thinking?" He chuckled knowingly. "Why does
that sound like you're about to spring a momentous announcement on me?"

"She's probably bringing home another stray animal," said Frannie lightly. "What is it this time, Bree?
A wounded platypus? A homeless carrier pigeon? A
dispossessed gopher?"

Bree scowled. "Don't make fun of me, Fran. I'm
serious."

"Serious?" Andrew echoed guardedly. "How serious?"

"Just a little bit serious," Bree said evasively.

Andrew looked her square in the eye. "Tell me, what
are you cooking up, my darling daughter?"

"Nothing, Daddy. It's just...this house has been so
empty since Cassie moved out. All three of us have
been feeling lonely, restless, at loose ends. It just
doesn't feel right, all these rooms with nobody to fill
them."

"And just who do you have in mind...to fill these
rooms?" asked Andrew, helping himself to the garlic
bread.

"Nobody in particular," said Bree, "except
maybe..."

"You might as well tell us," said Frannie. "Just say it, and we'll tell you if it's one of your crazy, impossible ideas."

Bree drew in a sharp breath. "There's a girl I've been counseling at the clinic—"

"Oh, no!" cried Frannie. "Last time it was a woman with a bunch of rowdy kids. They invaded the sunroom, helped themselves to my paint and pelted one another with wet clay. They made my bust of Cicero look like Donald Duck! In ten minutes they nearly destroyed my entire art studio."

"That was an unfortunate incident," Bree acknowledged in a regretful voice. "But this client has no children...yet."

"Yet?" quizzed Andrew. "Yet, as in...?"

"Three months."

"She's three months pregnant?" asked Frannie.

"No, her baby is due in three months."

"What's her story?" asked Andrew. "Her husband desert her?"

"Not exactly," said Bree. "She's a teenager. Almost nineteen. Her boyfriend broke up with her when he found out about the pregnancy, and it appears her parents want nothing to do with her. She's all alone in the world...and she won't admit it, but I know she's scared. You should see her, Daddy. Trying to act like it's no big deal when her world's caving in. She needs a place to stay where she feels loved and accepted."

Frannie poked at her spaghetti. "Can't she stay at the shelter, Bree?"

"It's mainly for battered wives. Besides, it's full."

Andrew cleared his throat. "Of course, the girl can stay here...if you think this is the place for her, Bree."

"I do, Daddy." Bree's voice rose with excitement.

"I really feel I can help her. *We* can help her. She may act blasé, even flippant at times, but I know she's hurting inside. She thinks everyone has condemned her."

"Well, then, let's pray we can show her the love of God."

"And she needs a job," said Bree. "Something to make her feel better about herself."

Frannie shook her head. "Who's going to hire a woman about to give birth?"

"I thought of that," said Bree. "That's why I was thinking that maybe we could—"

Andrew smiled grimly. "Oh, oh, I'm not sure I like that look in your eyes, daughter."

"But, Daddy, it'll be perfect. I've got it all figured out. Marnie can work for you."

"Marnie?"

"That's her name. Marnie Smith—although I think she made up the Smith part."

"What do you mean, she can work for me? I already have a secretary. You mean, work at the church?"

"No, Daddy. She can work right here. You're always saying you wish you had someone here at home to help with clerical work—correspondence, filing, research for your sermons. If she's staying here, anyway, she'll have time on her hands, waiting for her baby to come. She can earn money to give herself and her baby a fresh start. Please say you'll give her a chance."

Andrew reached across the table and patted his daughter's hand. "You win, dumpling. Have I ever said no when you've come home with one of your pet projects, your abandoned critters, your lost causes? Tell your young friend she has a home with us."

But even as Andrew said the words, a niggling worry crept in. He had an uneasy feeling that this needy young girl might change their lives in more ways than any of them expected.

their eyes met and the words vanishing with a sitting in the infant Rowley, feeling that the ready young girl might change their lives in more ways than any of them expected.

Chapter Two

Brianna brought Marnie home the next day, a balmy, late-June Saturday. The moment Marnie stepped inside the Rowlands' house, she did a double take. "Wow!" she said with grudging admiration. "This is awesome. Not glitzy, like a rich person's pad, but warm and homey. Like that retro Ozzie and Harriet stuff. A real home."

"Thanks," said Bree. "I think."

"I like it," Marnie went on, clutching a leather satchel in one hand and a canvas bag in the other. Tall and slender, with a coltish energy and grace, she looked like an ordinary teenager in her tank top and oversize bib overalls. No one would have guessed she was over six months pregnant.

"We can take your things directly up to your room, if you like," said Bree, nodding toward the stairs.

"No, I'll just set them here for now." Marnie dropped her belongings beside the staircase and ambled across the entryway, her stacked sandals clicking on the marble floor. "This place beats some dreary women's shelter." She drifted into the living room and gazed around at the overstuffed sofa and chairs, the oak furniture, and the bay windows letting in sunlight. They could see a profusion of color from the rosebushes lining the front yard.

Marnie flashed a lopsided smile. She had an oval face with sharp features—a nose too pointed, lips too full, teeth a bit too large. Her long, umber-brown hair looked a bit bedraggled, as if she had got up in the morning and absently smoothed it back from her forehead with her hands. Marnie's eyes—her most striking feature—were large, wide-set, shadowed at the corners, and a light spring-water blue. They seemed ageless, fathomless, melancholy, yet riveting, as if they were looking beyond the surface at something no one else could see.

"You sure your dad doesn't mind putting me up for a few months?" she asked in an offhand voice that failed to hide an undercurrent of anxiety.

"I'm sure," said Bree. "You stay as long as you need to."

Marnie managed a hard-edged chuckle. "I guess him being a minister makes him want to do nice things for people, like taking in the poor and homeless...and pregnant."

"He's a neat guy," said Bree. "Funny and warm and caring. You'll like him."

The two crossed the living room to the kitchen. It was roomy, with a sunny breakfast nook and garden window overlooking a sprawling backyard festooned with snow-white calla lilies, bright orange birds of paradise, pink azaleas in porcelain Ming pots, bougainvillea bushes, and a variety of tropical foliage.

"Are you hungry, Marnie?"

"Starved." She smiled grimly. "I'm eating for two, you know."

"Then, let's raid the fridge." Bree opened the refrigerator door and gazed inside. "Let's see. We've got all sorts of mysterious concoctions hidden in butter tubs, but I'm not sure we want to risk our lives by sampling them."

"I'm not fussy...as long as it's edible and not growing little fuzzy green things."

"I can't vouch for most of this stuff. My dad believes you should never throw anything out until it's clearly beyond redemption."

"Not a bad philosophy," noted Marnie with a hint of irony.

Bree nodded. "I never thought of it that way." She retrieved a large plastic container and peeked inside. "Tell you what. We have spaghetti left over from last night. My sister Frannie makes the best pasta dishes in the world. She does this thing with basil and oregano. I'm no cook, so I have no idea how she does it, but it's scrumptious."

Marnie sat down at the oak table. "I love spaghetti."

"Me, too. I'll zap us some in the microwave."

For the next half-hour they sat at the cozy table devouring the last of Frannie's spaghetti and sipping diet colas. They engaged in idle chitchat for a few minutes, discussing the weather, the house, even Brianna's job at the counseling center.

"What's it like giving out advice and helping people all day?" Marnie asked. "Does it make you feel like a saint? Joan of Arc or something?"

Brianna smiled. "It's scary and wonderful all at once."

"How so?"

"Scary when I think I'm responsible for people's lives. Wonderful when I know I've made life better for someone."

"Someone like me?"

"Yes. Someone like you."

Marnie lapsed into silence.

Brianna traced the rim of her cola glass. "I hope you don't mind, Marnie. I don't mean to intrude on your privacy, but now that you'll be living here, I'll need some information."

Marnie twisted a strand of chestnut hair. "Like what?"

"General stuff. About you. Your family. Your plans."

Marnie's tone was guarded. "What do you want to know?"

"For starters, where your home is."

"I filled out the papers you gave me."

"You listed a San Diego hotel."

"That's where I was staying. Until I ran out of money."

"What about your family? Where do they live?"

Marnie lowered her gaze. "That's not important."

"But it is. If we needed to reach them for some reason—"

"Leave them out of it," said Marnie sharply. "They have nothing to do with me anymore."

"Because you're pregnant? Did they force you to leave home? That's what you implied when you first came to see me."

Marnie sipped her cola. After a moment she looked up, her eyes shadowed, her lips tight, as if she were willing herself not to speak lest she say too much.

"Marnie, if I'm going to help you, I need to know the truth. Please. I'm on your side."

Marnie licked her chapped lips. Without makeup, she had a winsome, childlike face. She was still twisting her hair, so tightly that the tip of her finger had turned white. At last she met Brianna's gaze. "Truth is, my folks don't know I'm pregnant. When I started to show, I just wore frumpy clothes. No one could tell. I wouldn't even admit it to myself until a couple of months ago. When I told my boyfriend, Sam...Sam Dillard—we were both sophomores at San Diego State—when I told him, he told me to get rid of it. Just like that. He didn't even think twice about it. Just said he didn't want anything to do with a baby. It was my problem."

"Couldn't you tell your folks?"

"You kidding? My parents are...you'd have to know them...they're like, totally perfect. I mean, that's how they act, like they can do no wrong. You should see them. Rigid and unbending as a ruler. They expect perfection from everyone. No one can please them. Especially me." She gnawed on her lower lip, her gaze downcast. "Of course, my brother is another story."

"Your brother?"

"Eric. He's ten years older than me." Marnie pulled a thumb-worn snapshot from the pocket of her bib overalls and handed it to Bree. "I keep his picture close to my heart. Makes me feel like he's watching over me. Stupid, huh?"

"Not at all. That shows how special he must be." Bree studied the photograph. The face staring back at her was one of the most compelling and captivating she had ever seen. As finely honed as a Michelangelo sculpture. A valiant face reflecting a startling paradox of strength and vulnerability, melancholy and mischief.

And those dusky, half-moon eyes flashed lightning bolts straight into Bree's heart. They seemed to read her very thoughts. She couldn't tear her gaze from those eyes.

"This is…your brother?" she murmured, her voice catching. This was crazy. Her heart was doing a strange little pitter-pat dance. A self-conscious warmth spread across her face, flushing her cheeks, leaving her pleasantly dazed and distracted. What was wrong with her, reacting so viscerally? For heaven's sake, if a person could fall in love with a mere photograph, she just had!

"Cute, isn't he," said Marnie offhandedly.

"That's, uh…not the word for it." Bree forced her eyes from the snapshot. *Help me, Lord! I'm behaving like a tongue-tied schoolgirl.* "What's he like…your brother?"

"Oh, wow! He's like every girl wishes her brother would be." Marnie's eyes grew misty, as if she were glimpsing distant, faded memories. "He was always looking out for me…always there when I needed him. When I was a little girl, he carried me around in one of those little snuggly things. On his chest. Like I was a papoose or something. Can you imagine? Him a big teenage boy carrying around his little sister? He took me everywhere. To his ball games and track meets. On bike rides and hikes. He always fixed me hot dogs and macaroni and cheese—his absolute favorites. When I was sick, he brought his friends in to do stupid animal imitations. Bugs Bunny. Donald Duck. We'd laugh our silly heads off. But what was so cool…he made me feel like one of the gang. He was never ashamed of me."

Bree struggled to find her voice. She was falling harder by the minute. "He sounds like a…a wonderful guy."

"The best." Marnie cupped her cola glass with her

palms. "He's a lawyer now. One of the good guys. Not one of those greedy dudes chasing million-dollar law-suits." Marnie met Bree's gaze. "Actually, he's a lot like you, Brianna. Always helping people, championing some cause for the poor and downtrodden."

"Then, why didn't you tell him about the baby?"

"And see the disappointment in his eyes? No way! He's the only one who ever stood up for me. When my folks got on my case, Eric always came to my defense. He's the only person who ever really believed in me, who thought I was worth something."

"Then all the more reason to take him into your confidence."

"No way!" Marnie blinked back rising tears. "Don't you get it? I don't ever want to stop being special to him."

Bree sat back and gave a relenting sigh. Reluctantly, she handed the photo back to Marnie. "Okay, if that's how you want it. But he sounds like a fabulous brother."

"He is. You'd love him."

I already do! The thought stunned Bree. How could a stranger's face leave her feeling so shaken and flustered?

"Trouble is, he's too dedicated to his work. It's his whole life. Doesn't even have a girlfriend." Marnie eyed Brianna knowingly. "I bet you're the same way, aren't you. Too busy with your work to have a special guy?"

Brianna grimaced. She might consider having a special guy if he were anything like Marnie's brother. "We're talking about your life, Marnie," she said evasively. "Not mine."

"But it's true, isn't it? No boyfriend?"

Bree assumed her quasi-professional voice. "That's how I like it, Marnie. No man complicating my life."

"Smart lady!" Marnie's blue eyes darkened. She resolutely mopped back her hair with one hand. "If I'd had that attitude, I wouldn't be in this mess now."

"About your brother," said Bree. *Tell me everything,* she wanted to say, but resisted the impulse. "You don't want him to find out you're pregnant. But you can't just disappear without raising suspicions. Won't your parents be looking for you?"

"No. Never in a million years."

"How can you be so sure?"

Marnie flashed a sly smile. "I got it all arranged."

"Arranged?"

For a moment Marnie looked as if she couldn't quite decide whether or not to confide in Brianna. Finally she said, "Here's the scoop. My girlfriend from school got a scholarship to study in Europe this summer. I told my parents I got a scholarship, too. Said I was going with her."

"To Europe?"

"Yeah. You should have seen how happy they were, thinking I got this humongous scholarship worth thousands of dollars. Thinking I was going off to study in Europe. What a hoot! That's the picture they have of me—the daughter they want. Not some stupid girl who gets knocked up by her first boyfriend."

"Your family really thinks you're in Europe studying?"

"Yeah. Would you believe? I even wrote postcards for my friend to mail from Europe. Me raving to my mom and dad about what an awesome time I'm having in Paris. And all the while I'm right here, a half-hour away, in some minister's house…a charity case, waiting to have a baby.''

''You're no charity case. You'll be earning your keep.''

''For sure? How?''

''I told you. Doing secretarial work for my dad.''

''I figured you just said that so I wouldn't feel so bad about sponging off your family.''

''No, my father can really use your help. You can type letters…you did say you can type, right?''

Marnie nodded. ''Yeah, that's one thing I'm good at.''

''And maybe help him with some research on his sermons.''

''Sermons?'' Marnie's eyes widened. ''Listen, girl, I'm not one of those religious types. I mean, my family went to church now and then, but it was more for show, you know?''

''Marnie, I'm not asking if you—''

''Okay, so my brother's into this church thing. He goes to a church my parents totally disapprove of. What a hoot, huh? I went with him once. They meet in a school. No piano or choir. Just a ragtag band. Guitars and drums. Doesn't matter what you wear—jeans, tees, sandals. No one cares if you're rich or poor.''

Bree finished her cola. ''So tell me. Did you enjoy going?''

''Yeah, I did. Weird, huh? The people were kinda nice—down to earth, you know?'' Marnie poked at her last strands of spaghetti. ''Eric wanted me to keep going, but I was with Sam at the time, and Sam wanted no part of church.''

Bree met her gaze. ''The truth is, Marnie, while

you're living here, my dad expects you to attend church with us."

She shrugged. "I can handle it. Your dad's the preacher, right? If he's as cool as you say, it shouldn't be so bad."

"You might even like it. My dad has a way of telling the truth so you want to hear more."

Marnie glanced around, as if expecting someone to appear suddenly. "Maybe I should get my stuff upstairs before your family gets home."

"No hurry," said Bree. "My dad's at the church, Frannie's teaching an art class at San Diego State, and Ruggs, our dog, who rules the house, is in the backyard, probably burying his favorite bones in the flower garden."

Marnie laughed lightly. "I love dogs. But my parents wouldn't let me have one. Said an animal would mess up their house. But if I had my own place, I'd have a dozen dogs running around. And maybe a couple of cats, too."

Now it was Bree's turn to laugh. "Sounds like a regular menagerie. How about a bird? And monkeys are fun."

Marnie stifled a chuckle. Her eyes were merry again, her cheeks ruddy. "Guess I'd need a farm, huh? Cows, horses, pigs, sheep. Nice little place far from California, where the land goes on forever and the stars are so bright they wink at you."

"Sounds marvelous," said Bree, "if that's the kind of life you're looking for."

Marnie twisted another strand of hair. "I don't know what I'm looking for."

"You must have some plans...dreams..."

"Nothing. Except get through the summer and have my baby."

"What then?" asked Bree. "Will you take your baby home?"

Marnie looked up reproachfully, her eyes welling with tears. "I can't. My family can never know. My baby...I'm giving her up. I gotta find a good family to adopt her." Marnie sat forward, her elbows on the table, her voice filled with sudden urgency. "You've gotta help me find a good home for my baby. A family to love her and accept her as she is, not make her feel she can never be good enough. Will you help me?"

Brianna reached across the table and clasped Marnie's hands. "I'll do what I can. But maybe you'll change your mind and decide to keep your baby."

Marnie's eyes hardened to an icy blue. "No, I can't keep her. I've got to pretend she never existed. I've got to go home at the end of the summer and go back to school and act like nothing ever happened. I've got to get my education and pray someday I can make my parents proud of me."

"You're asking a lot of yourself, Marnie. Are you sure about your parents? Maybe once they got used to the idea, they'd welcome a baby into the family."

Marnie pushed back her plate. "Not my parents! They don't want me...and they sure don't want my baby."

"Okay, forget I mentioned it." Bree stood up and took the plates and glasses over to the sink. "If you're ready, Marnie, I'll show you to your room."

Marnie hoisted herself from the chair and suddenly clutched her abdomen. "Oh, wow!"

Brianna pivoted. "What is it? What's wrong?"

"The baby." Marnie moved her hand slowly over

her rounded belly. "Man, she's kicking like mad. Feel, Brianna."

Gently Marnie placed Brianna's hand on the spot where the baby was moving. Sure enough, Bree could feel the fluttering kicks against her palm. Rhythmic little thumps. The sensation was amazing...as if this tiny, unseen child were reaching out to her, trying to make contact, entreating her for help.

Don't worry, little one, Bree promised silently. I'm going to take care of you and your mommy. I'll make sure you have a wonderful family to love you...if it's the last thing I do!

Chapter Three

Andrew Rowlands hadn't been on a real date in months. And this wasn't really a date, either, he reminded himself. On this balmy August evening he and Juliana Pagliarulo were having dinner together at a little Italian bistro in Del Mar. Nothing to it. Longtime friends simply having a pleasant evening together.

Then why was his heart pounding now with excitement as he gazed across the table at her? Why were his palms perspiring? Why did he feel like a teenage boy out on his first date? It wasn't as if he and Juliana hadn't had plenty of dinners together before. Hey, they were practically related, now that her son was married to his daughter. Andrew had even kissed Juliana in the moonlight a time or two. They had talked about having a future together, and then they had decided...*he* had decided...that they should just be friends—no entanglements, no commitments, no romance. Just friends.

The only problem was that since he had made that decision, he couldn't get Juliana out of his head.

Couldn't stop remembering those kisses. Couldn't stop yearning for more.

For six long years he had managed to remain faithful to Mandy, to her memory. He had convinced himself there would never be another woman in his life. He had had the perfect marriage. Okay, not perfect, but as close as two flawed human beings could get. Even after Mandy's death he had still felt a connection with her. He had done an amazing job of keeping her alive in his head, in his heart. His love for her had never dimmed.

But lately, his emotions were betraying him. He couldn't summon memories of Mandy the way he used to, couldn't visualize her face, her eyes, her smile. It was as if she were slowly, inevitably retreating from him, quietly vanishing into the shadows. How could that be? How could he be losing her again?

Whatever it took, he couldn't let that happen. He couldn't stand to lose Mandy twice in one lifetime. Hadn't he already grieved enough? Hadn't he remained stalwart and unshakable in the face of grief? It had taken more strength than he had imagined to reconcile himself to living with mere memories, but he had done it. Had become surprisingly comfortable, in fact.

But now everything was changing. A wellspring of long-suppressed emotions was erupting in his soul, mushrooming up, supplanting his placid memories of Mandy, replacing them with confusing feelings, unexpected yearnings, unsettling desires. And they all focused on one woman—the lovely, loquacious Juliana Pagliarulo.

"Andrew? Andrew, are you still here?"

Startled, he gazed over the flickering candles at Juliana. She was wearing a stylish, red, belted sheath that accentuated her hourglass figure, and her raven-black hair was swept up in an elegant twist. The candlelight danced in her dark, sultry eyes and gave her bronze complexion a breathtaking radiance.

He cleared his throat, trying to compose himself. "I'm sorry, Juliana. What did you say?"

She leaned forward, a smile teasing her red lips. "I said, here I am having dinner with a very handsome man, and he's a million miles away. Am I losing my touch?"

He grinned, red-faced. "No, not at all. My mind wandered for a moment. I apologize."

"Dare I ask where it wandered?"

He flinched. He didn't want Juliana thinking he was still mooning over his dead wife after all these years, especially when he was on a date with her.

Before he could respond, she murmured gently, "Is it Mandy?"

He lowered his gaze. This lady could read him like a book. "Foolish of me, isn't it? How can I be thinking about the past when the present company is so delightfully enchanting?"

Her smile widened, a slow, mysterious Mona Lisa smile. "How can I take offense when you say such endearing things?"

Their repartee was interrupted when the waitress brought their Caesar salads. Andrew reached across the table for Juliana's hand and held it as he bowed his head and asked a blessing on the food. They ate in silence for a moment; then, making conversation, Andrew asked, "So how are the newlyweds doing?"

Juliana blotted her lips with her linen napkin. "Oh, Andrew, they are so in love. You should see them together. They have eyes only for each other."

Andrew nodded, beaming. "I'm glad they're happy."

He didn't want to admit it to Juliana, but he had been a little concerned about his daughter moving into the Pagliarulo estate and beginning her marriage with her mother-in-law and sister-in-law already in residence. With two other women there, Cassie could hardly be the woman of the house. Cautiously he ventured, "How is it working out with all of you under one roof?"

Juliana waved her hand gracefully in the air. "Oh, there is no trouble. We all get along very well. Sometimes I cook, sometimes Cassie cooks, sometimes we cook together. But if you ask me, I think she is just as happy when I take charge."

"Cassie never was one to cultivate her culinary skills. She was always glad Frannie did the cooking in our house."

"Well, she and Antonio live such busy lives, I don't mind taking care of the household chores."

"Just the same," warned Andrew, "don't let her take advantage of your kindness. One of these days she has to learn what being a homemaker is all about."

"Oh, I'm sure she will learn in time. But for now my son and your daughter feel as if they are still on their honeymoon."

Andrew finished his salad and set down his fork. "How is your daughter adjusting to the new living arrrangements?"

"Belina is very happy to have Cassie living with us now. The two have become good friends. Now that Belina is out of her wheelchair and walking again, she spends little time in her room. She's discovering a whole new world outside the walls of our home. Cassie and Belina go shopping and take walks together. Cassie has even convinced Belina to enroll at the university."

"Really? I'm amazed."

"So was I. It's hard to believe my daughter who refused to leave her room a year ago is taking classes and meeting people."

"I know how much that means to you," said Andrew. "And I'm glad Cassie could have a part in helping her."

"A very large part, Andrew. I am so grateful to her."

They paused as the waitress brought Juliana's manicotti and his veal parmigiana and replenished their basket of garlic bread.

Juliana helped herself to the bread and broke off a crust. "Andrew, the doctors have set a date for Belina's surgery."

"Surgery?"

"The side of her face where she was burned in the accident...they have a new technique to remove scar tissue and replace it with skin from another part of her body. So, if all goes well, she will no longer have to live with her disfigurement."

"Wonderful," said Andrew. He had liked Belina from the first time they met; he had seen her potential and felt her pain over her scars and physical handicap. Now she was walking again and soon would be as beautiful outside as she was inside.

"Will you come with me to the hospital?" asked Juliana softly. "When Belina goes to surgery?"

Andrew reached across the table for Juliana's hand and squeezed it firmly. "Of course I will. You know I'll be there."

Tears welled in Juliana's eyes, but she smiled brightly in spite of them. "I had hoped that's what you would say."

He sat forward with a confidential air, as if he were about to impart a secret. "You know, Juliana, that I will be there for you whenever you need me. Just say the word.'' He felt a sudden impulse to say more, to confess how much he cared for her, how much he needed her, how he was wrong to let their blossoming relationship slip away, but he caught himself and nearly bit his lower lip to keep the words back. Juliana had enough to deal with, without him getting unduly sentimental and burdening her with impossible expectations.

How could he suggest they resume a romantic relationship when it couldn't possibly lead anywhere? It wasn't as if they were two lovesick teenagers who could run off and get married and forge a single destiny for themselves. He and Juliana had lived very different lives; they both had obligations, responsibilities that neither could ask the other to surrender. They each had a well-established household to run. Juliana had her daughter to care for, and Andrew had two of his still at home.

He couldn't imagine asking Juliana to give up her glamorous, independent life in her fancy Del Mar estate to marry him and move into his comfortable but admittedly provincial home. And the idea of the feisty, flamboyant Juliana Pagliarulo performing the humble duties of a minister's wife was preposterous, prompting him to laugh aloud.

''What's so funny, Andrew?'' asked Juliana with a quizzical smile on her lovely face.

He cleared his throat self-consciously. ''Funny?''

''You just laughed, as if someone had told you a joke. What were you thinking about?''

He rubbed his jaw awkwardly, his face warming with embarrassment. Juliana had caught him. There was no way he could tell her the truth—*I was laughing at the idea of you being a minister's wife*—and no way he could lie. All he could do was stall or divert the conversation. "How is your manicotti?" he enquired.

She smiled knowingly. "Delicious. But you are avoiding my question. Why did you laugh suddenly?"

He shook his head. "It was nothing...a silly thought. Okay, you asked for it. The truth is, I was thinking about us...how different we are."

"Is that so bad?" she asked in her most alluring voice.

"I suppose not. Opposites attract, as they say."

"Is that true for us, Andrew? The attraction part, I mean."

He poked absently at his food. "You know the answer to that one, Juliana."

"I thought I did," she murmured, lowering her gaze. He couldn't miss the disappointment in her voice.

They both slipped into an unsettling silence that made Andrew's stomach churn. He had intended this to be a casual, uncomplicated evening, some good food and pleasant conversation between friends, nothing more; surely nothing heavy or awkward. And now they were both precariously close to dredging up unresolved emotions and unfulfilled expectations. Neither had ever admitted it, but he knew they both wanted more from this relationship.

And they both knew it was impossible.

Try as he might, Andrew couldn't think of a thing to say to neutralize the tension-filled moment.

Thankfully, Juliana recovered quickly and flashed a brilliant smile. "Andrew, you haven't told me how things are at your house."

"My house?"

"Yes. With Brianna and your new houseguest. What's her name?"

"Marnie. Marnie Smith…if that's her real name."

"Why would she mislead you?"

"Her family doesn't know she's pregnant."

"I see." Juliana took another slice of garlic bread. "The girl is working for you, isn't she? Or did I hear wrong?"

"You heard right. She's doing secretarial work for me at home. Letters, filing, research. A good worker and a genuinely nice girl. Pleasant. Kind. Caring. Plays a mean game of Monopoly. To tell you the truth, I'll miss her when she goes."

"And when is that?"

"After the baby comes. It's due early in September. From what Bree tells me, Marnie will give the baby up for adoption and then return home, supposedly with no one the wiser."

Juliana shook her head, her eyes clouding. "What a painful thing to do. She must be a very brave girl to carry a baby for nine months and then be willing to let it go."

"She feels she has no choice. Meanwhile, both she and Brianna are caught up in the pregnancy. Bree is even taking Lamaze classes. She plans to be Marnie's coach."

"Oh, Andrew, I can't imagine it. Childbirth is so different these days. Girls have such modern ideas."

"Actually, I find it a little disconcerting. Brianna is so excited, you'd think she's the one having the baby."

"From what you've told me, she's always been the little mother, bringing home lost and needy animals… and people."

"That's my daughter," said Andrew. "Trying to mend the hurts of the whole world. But this is different."

"How so?"

"I'm not sure." He drummed his fingers on the table. "I haven't said this to anyone, but I'm worried about Brianna."

"Why?"

"I don't know. It's just...well, she's become so emotionally involved with Marnie and her baby. I'm afraid Bree is going to feel a real loss when they leave."

"She'll handle it, Andrew. Look how strong she's been all these years since her mother died."

"You're right. So why do I have this nagging fear that one more significant loss might send her over the edge?"

"You don't really believe that, do you?"

"Not that she would be a basket case. But another loss could make her erect more fences. She's thrown herself heart and soul into helping others, but she has no personal life. She rarely dates. How is she going to find a suitable husband if she keeps a lock on her heart?"

Juliana laughed lightly. "Oh, Andrew, you're playing matchmaker again, just like you did with Cassie and Antonio. Haven't you learned your lesson? It doesn't work. We are fortunate that our children found each other in spite of our fussing and scheming. You must trust your daughter to do what's right for her, and trust God to bring the right young man into her life at the proper time."

"In other words, you're saying I should be patient? I should just sit back and let whatever happens, happen?"

"Yes. You are a man of faith. Have faith in your daughter."

"I'm trying." Andrew lapsed into silence. What he

didn't want to tell Juliana was that his misgivings were growing every day. He couldn't even say why. He just had an uneasy feeling about Marnie and her baby. He sensed there was trouble ahead, and that somehow his caring, unsuspecting Brianna was going to be in the thick of it.

Now, if he could just figure out a way to protect his darling daughter before it was too late.

Chapter Four

It was a lazy Saturday afternoon, and the golden August sun was flooding the Rowlands' house with shimmering light and warmth. An old-time movie was playing on the big-screen TV and a half-eaten bag of microwave popcorn lay on the family room floor where Brianna and Marnie were ensconced, practicing Marnie's breathing exercises. Ruggs crouched between them, panting, too, his furry chest heaving.

"Hooo-hooo-heee!" Marnie puffed, while Ruggs licked his chops, dangled his tongue, and bobbed his head, huffing like a trooper.

Marnie laughed. "Ruggs has this breathing thing down better than we do."

Brianna rubbed the shaggy dog's ears, laughing, too. "This old boy always was good at wheezing, but not much else."

"And he doesn't even have to go through labor," Marnie exclaimed, sitting back in her loose dungarees and patting her ample middle. "Oh, man, these Braxton-Hicks contractions are getting bad. Can you believe? I've got just one month left to get this Lamaze thing right.''

''You're doing fine,'' Bree assured her as she reached for the popcorn.

And it was true. In the two months since Marnie had come to stay, she had blossomed in every way—physically, of course, as her pregnancy advanced, but also emotionally and spiritually. She wasn't the same edgy, brooding girl who had first come to the counseling center seeking a place of refuge. Now she was a cheerful, welcome member of the Rowlands' household, eagerly entering into family activities, helping Brianna's father in his home office, attending church services, and whispering excitedly whenever Reverend Rowlands used some of her research in his sermons.

Marnie was still chuckling as Ruggs edged over beside her, panting heavily. He nudged her hand with his wet nose, seeking another ear massage. Marnie pulled the big hairy oaf into her arms and gave him a bear hug. ''You silly old dog! I should make you my coach. Wouldn't you give the doctors a run for their money in the delivery room!''

''No way,'' said Bree, scooping up a handful of fluffy popcorn kernels. ''I'm your one and only coach.''

''And don't you forget it!'' Marnie's expression grew serious and her blue eyes glistened. ''I don't know how I could get through this without you, Bree.''

''You don't have to. I'm with you all the way.'' After a pause, Brianna added, ''And you have the Lord, too, you know.''

Marnie ran her fingers through her long chestnut hair, her countenance darkening. ''Do I?''

Bree nodded. ''If you ask Him, He'll be there for you. He loves you, Marnie.''

Marnie lowered her gaze, absently rubbing Ruggs's floppy ears. "I'm not like you and your family, Bree, always doing the right thing." Her voice was quiet, tentative. "Being religious comes naturally to all of you."

Bree let out a whoop. "Is that how you see us? You haven't been looking closely. We have our problems, our faults, our squabbles. We make mistakes. We don't always see eye to eye."

"But you have your faith. I see it in everything you do."

"And you can have that, too, Marnie."

She shook her head. "No, I'm not good enough. Look at me, the way I've messed up my life. Pregnant, alone, running from my family. What would God want with a loser like me?"

Bree put the popcorn bag aside and scooted closer to Marnie. Gently she squeezed her shoulder. "If you've been listening to my dad's sermons, you know God doesn't accept us because of how good we are. None of us, no matter how hard we try, can ever measure up to God's glory."

"I know that, but..."

"Then you know the rest of the story, too. God loved us so much He sent His Son to die for us. Jesus paid for our sins with His own life so we could have fellowship with God. All we have to do is accept His gift. Invite Christ into our lives."

"I want to," Marnie conceded, "but it seems...too easy."

"It is easy," said Bree. "Anyone...everyone can do it, no matter how bad they've been in the past, no matter how many mistakes they've made. Christ can wash away their sins and make them clean, as if they'd never sinned. Sometimes, when I think about it, I get excited just imagining how much God must love us to do what He does for us. Think of it, Marnie. When we trust Him, God accepts us as His own precious children.''

Marnie's fingers still kneaded the fur around Ruggs's ears. ''It sounds way cool, Bree. But my own parents would disown me for messing up. So how can I expect God not to condemn me?''

''Because God says He will remember our sins no more, and God doesn't lie.'' Bree smoothed Marnie's long, dark hair.

In these two short months she had come to love Marnie like a sister. Somehow she had to make the road ahead easier for her. ''Believe me, Marnie, placing your faith in God and walking with Him day by day is the most amazing experience you can have on this earth. Think of it. Feeling cherished and loved by the God of the universe. Nothing else even comes close to that.''

Marnie sat quietly for a long while, rocking, one hand on her rounded belly, the other smoothing Ruggs's fur. Her lower lip trembled. Finally she looked up with bright, tearful eyes and said, ''Help me, Bree. Help me pray and say the right words, so I can know God the way you do.''

On Monday afternoon, the last week of August, Marnie asked Bree if she could borrow her car for a couple of hours to take care of an important personal matter. Bree agreed, nearly dying of curiosity, but as she handed Marnie the keys she refrained from asking questions. If Marnie wanted her to know her business, she would tell her when the time was right.

The time was right that very evening. After dinner, while Brianna's father retired to his study and Frannie escaped to the sunroom to work on her latest sculpture,

Marnie and Bree cleared the table and loaded the dishwasher. They worked in a companionable silence for a while. Then Marnie broke the stillness.

"Bree, I got a favor to ask."

Bree kept working. "A favor? Sure, what is it?"

"It's a big one."

Bree stopped and looked at Marnie. She didn't like the seriousness in her tone. Something was wrong. "How big a favor are we talking about?"

"The biggest," said Marnie with a little catch in her voice. "I...I want you to keep my baby."

Brianna stared dumbfounded at Marnie. Surely she hadn't heard right—and yet from the poignant, sad-hopeful look on Marnie's face, Bree knew she had. "Keep your baby?"

Marnie nodded, sudden tears rolling from her eyes. "Please, Bree, say you will! I'll owe you forever."

Bree wiped her hands and sat down at the table. "Why me?"

Marnie sat across from her and leaned forward with a fierce urgency. "Because you care about me...and I know you would love my baby."

"I already do, but..." Bree shook her head, her thoughts reeling. "Look at me. I'm a single career woman with a full-time job, and not a husband in sight. And babies...I don't know the first thing about them. You want your baby to have a real family, parents who would be devoted to her, a father and a mother."

"That's what I thought at first. But now I know your family is just what my baby needs. You all love each other so much. You don't put each other down. Your house is great—the happiest place I've ever known."

"I-I'm glad you've been happy here," Bree stam-

mered. "We all want to help out and be here for you.
But that doesn't mean this is the place for your baby."

"But it is, Bree!" Marnie brushed awkwardly at a
tear. She was about to become a mother, and she herself
looked like a lost child, a forlorn little waif, her tousled
dark hair framing her desolate face, her lower lip jutting
out in a pout. "This is totally the place for my baby. I
can't take her home. I can't let my family know about
her. Don't you get it? Once she's born, I can't ever see
my baby again. But giving her away to strangers...I just
can't do it."

"Then don't, Marnie. Keep your baby. Take her
home."

"No way, Bree. If my folks got hold of her, they'd
make her feel as bad about herself as I've always felt.
But if you took her, I'd know she was happy. I could
picture her here in your house, surrounded by love.
You'd teach her about God's love, too. Knowing she
had you, I could let her go."

Bree rubbed at a spot on the polished oak table.
Somehow she had to make Marnie see how impossible
her request was. But nothing she could say would dissuade Marnie while she was in such an agitated state.
Maybe it was best to drop the subject for now. In a day
or two Marnie would come to her senses.

"You don't think I mean it, do you," Marnie challenged.

"I think you're feeling a little emotional right now,
but when you've had time to think things through—"

"I won't change my mind." Marnie stood up. "I'll
prove how serious I am." She strode out of the kitchen,
and Bree heard her hurried steps on the stairs. A minute
later she was back. She slapped several official-looking
documents on the table.

Bree stared blankly at the forms, not really seeing them. "What are these?"

Marnie sat back down and said solemnly, "They're legal papers. It's official. I'm relinquishing my parental rights...and making you my baby's temporary legal guardian. Later you can file a petition to adopt her."

Bree stared incredulously at Marnie. "What have you done?"

Marnie smoothed out the papers. "I...I saw your father's attorney, Martin Cohen. Now he's my attorney, too."

"But how?"

"I got his name from your dad. I figured he must be a good person. Someone who could help me. So I phoned him and told him what I wanted to do, and he drew up the papers. I met with him today to sign them."

"But how did you know how to go about it?"

Marnie smiled wanly. "You forget. My brother is a lawyer. I'm not my brother's sister for nothing. I learned a lot from him, just listening and paying attention. I want all my bases covered. I even had Mr. Cohen contact Sam, my baby's father. Sam signed off his rights, too, so it's all settled, Bree."

"No, it isn't!" Brianna exclaimed, pushing the papers back at Marnie. "You can't do this!"

"I've already done it." Marnie sat with her arms wrapped protectively around her enormous middle. She looked so forlorn and vulnerable, and yet absolutely determined. "The papers are legal, Bree. Sam and I already signed them. I've designated you to be my baby's guardian. If you'll accept her, she's yours."

Brianna shook her head, dazed. She felt like the fabled Alice at the Mad Hatter's tea party. The moment struck her as illogical, preposterous. "I can't take your baby, Marnie."

Marnie scooped up the papers and held them to her breast. She looked crestfallen. "You don't have to decide now. There's still time. Just think about it."

"I can't promise anything..."

Marnie's eyes were searing, desolate. "If you can't keep her, at least help me find a loving family to adopt her."

Bree nodded, her relief tinged with guilt. "Yes, of course, I'll be glad to do that. Don't worry, Marnie. We'll find the right family for your baby."

There didn't seem to be much else to say after that. Marnie was clearly disappointed by Bree's attitude, but what could Brianna do? What could she say? She was certainly in no position to raise someone else's child.

They both went to bed early, Marnie complaining of mounting discomfort and exhaustion. Bree had a feeling the brooding girl just wanted to be alone to nurse her disappointment.

Sometime in the night Brianna heard a knock on her door. She sat bolt upright in bed and peered through the darkness as the door creaked open and Marnie peeked inside. "Bree, something's wrong," she said with alarm. "Something weird's happening. I went to the bathroom and there was a gush of water. I...I think my baby's coming."

Bree threw back her covers and jumped out of bed. "Get dressed. I'll wake my dad. He'll drive us to the hospital."

By the time Marnie was checked into her hospital room, it was nearly 5:00 a.m. Her contractions were coming five minutes apart.

"It's too soon," Marnie lamented as she paced the

floor in her shapeless maternity gown, massaging her distended abdomen. "My baby's not due for another month."

The nurse, a lean, bony woman with short, gray hair, jotted something on Marnie's chart. "Your baby's eager to make his appearance, dear. But don't worry. He has a good, strong heartbeat. Try to relax. You're both going to do fine."

Marnie kept pacing. "How long will it be?"

"Could be hours yet. But walking will help your labor progress. Dr. Packard will be in to check you shortly. And I'll be back from time to time to monitor your contractions. Meanwhile, remember, no food, no water. Just ice chips."

The next few hours crept by with an exhausting tedium. Bree finally sent her father home to catch a few winks of sleep. But she stayed by Marnie's side, timing her contractions, massaging her shoulders and back, and walking the floor with her in a slow, strolling saunter— the awkward, agonizing dance of the laboring mother. When the contractions came, Bree held Marnie up, their arms entwined as they went through their paces. When the pains got too bad, she helped Marnie climb into the large hospital bed and reminded her to practice her breathing exercises. Hoo-hoo-hee! Hoo-hoo-hee!

At about 10:00 a.m., Dr. Packard announced that Marnie was dilated to nine centimeters and in transition. Two attendants helped her onto the gurney and wheeled her into the delivery room, while Brianna slipped a sterile gown over her clothes. With pounding heart, she entered the stark gray room with its pale moons of light.

"I'm so glad you're with me," Marnie whispered through clenched teeth as she gripped Bree's hand. She was trembling, her hand cold as ice, her face and hair damp with perspiration. "Help me, okay? I'm not doing so well with the breathing."

"I'm right here." Brianna positioned herself by Marnie's head. "I'm not going anywhere. We're going to do this together."

Marnie tensed. "Oh no, I've got to push!"

"It's okay," Dr. Packard assured her. "On the next contraction, give it all you've got."

After pushing through several contractions, Marnie lay back, panting, exhausted, tears coursing down her cheeks. "I can't do it. I just can't!"

"Yes, you can," said Dr. Packard. "Rest a minute, then we'll try again."

"I'm too tired."

Brianna stroked Marnie's forehead, gently smoothing back the damp tendrils of hair. "You're doing great, Marnie. Almost there. Don't give up."

Dr. Packard moved in closer, working deftly, one hand pressing Marnie's abdomen. "Okay, young lady, here we go. Push! That's it. More. Come on. You can do it! Good, good, good! You've got it! The baby's head is crowning. Okay, relax, take a deep cleansing breath, and then one more good push should do it."

Marnie's face turned red with pushing. She made a low, guttural sound and squeezed Bree's hand until Bree winced with pain.

Suddenly a baby's choking, gurgling, high-pitched squall filled the room. As a nurse suctioned the infant's mouth and nose, Dr. Packard bent forward, his brown eyes crinkling above his surgical mask. "You've done the hard part, Marnie. We have the head. Now push that baby out."

On the next contraction the baby's shiny body slipped out effortlessly. The child raged in the doctor's sturdy hands—the most beautiful music Brianna had ever heard—followed closely by Marnie's laughter. "I did it, Bree. What a hoot! My baby! Look, my baby!"

"It's a girl! She's a little one, but she wants the whole world to know she's here." Dr. Packard placed the slick, squirming infant on Marnie's chest and proceeded to cut the umbilical cord. Both Marnie and Bree stared transfixed at the bawling baby.

Marnie wept. "She's gorgeous, isn't she, Bree?"

Suddenly Brianna was laughing and crying, too. "She's a little angel. Absolutely perfect!"

The baby was more than perfect. She was like a miracle. Tiny, yet plump and pink, with round, red cheeks and silky blonde hair on the top of her adorable head. And, flailing her taut little arms and legs, she was bursting with marvelous energy and life.

"I'm calling her Charity," said Marnie breathlessly. "Because I want her life to be filled with love."

"It will be," said Bree. "Who could help but love her?"

The baby began to gasp and sputter.

"Time to weigh her in, warm her up and get her in her Isolette," said Dr. Packard.

A nurse swept the infant up in her arms and took her to a table across the room.

Marnie leaned up on her elbows, her face pale, her blue eyes blazing. "Where are you taking my baby? Is she okay?"

Dr. Packard placed a soothing hand on Marnie's arm. "She's small and may need some extra attention. As a precaution, we'll put her in an Isolette and send her to the intensive care nursery, where the pediatrician can examine her."

Moments later, as an attendant wheeled the portable

crib out of the room, Marnie looked urgently at Brianna. "Go with her. I don't want my baby being alone. Stay with her. Watch over her."

Bree hesitated. "I can't leave you yet, Marnie."

"Yes, please, go! Make sure my baby's okay."

Dr. Packard nodded. "Go ahead. We shouldn't be much longer."

Brianna felt an odd reluctance to go—but Marnie had insisted, so what else was she to do? She leaned over, caressed Marnie's face and kissed her cheek. She drew back, startled. Marnie's skin felt strangely clammy, her forehead feverish. Her face was pallid, her eyes glazed. "Are you okay, Marnie?"

"Never better," Marnie mumbled thickly, her eyelids heavy.

"I love you," Bree whispered. Gently she squeezed Marnie's hand, then crossed the room to the door.

"Tell Charity...her mommy loves her," Marnie murmured with a weary smile. Her voice was faint, her breathing labored. "Tell her..."

Dr. Packard broke in. "Marnie, I need another push. I'm delivering the placenta. That's a girl. We're almost done."

Brianna lingered by the door, watching, as Marnie laid her head back and closed her eyes. She was trembling so fiercely that her teeth chattered. "I don't feel well," she whispered. "My chest hurts. And I'm so cold."

"Her pulse is rapid," warned the nurse.

Dr. Packard's voice erupted in a strangled bark. "Confound it! She's hemorrhaging!" He sprang into action, kneading Marnie's abdomen as another nurse joined them. "Massage the uterus! Come on! Vigorously! Don't stop!"

"It's not helping, Doctor."

"Try bimanual compression!" Dr. Packard muttered something under his breath about the placenta separating prematurely. His voice was urgent, shrill. "She'll need a transfusion!"

"Doctor, she's going into shock."

"Get a cardiologist in here! We need help!"

"Doctor, what's wrong?" Brianna broke away from the door and crossed the room to Marnie. "Is she okay?"

Dr. Packard looked at Brianna as if he had forgotten she was there. His face ignited with vexation. "Get her out of here! Now!"

Before Brianna could protest, an attendant—a tall young man in green scrubs—swiftly ushered her out the door and pointed the way to the critical care nursery.

Bree held her ground, her gaze riveted on the closed double doors of the delivery room. "What about Marnie? Will she be all right?"

"They're doing all they can." The attendant looked as shaken as she. "Go look after the baby," he said miserably, as if he already knew the news would be bad. "That's what she wanted, isn't it?"

Brianna nodded, her thoughts reeling. "I've got to call my father. He needs to be here." They were all going to need him...his presence, his comfort, his prayers.

The baby was in trouble. Marnie was in trouble. And Brianna couldn't imagine losing either one of them.

Chapter Five

"I'm sorry, Miss Rowlands. We did everything we could." Dr. Packard's small dark eyes glistened starkly in his lean, blanched face as one corner of his mouth twitched. He was still wearing his surgical greens, but he seemed slighter—his frame more diminutive, his manner less commanding—than Brianna had perceived him during surgery an hour ago. It struck her suddenly that he was as shocked and unnerved as she.

"Marnie's...dead?" Bree repeated numbly, as if she might somehow prompt a different response. It couldn't be! Baby Charity was hardly more than an hour old, and already she had lost her mommy. Bree swayed, the air sucked from her lungs, the fluorescent lights glaring against her rising tears. How could her dear Marnie, the girl she had nurtured and laughed with and loved as a sister, be gone so swiftly, so senselessly?

"We'll need to contact her next-of-kin," Dr. Packard was saying. "I understand she was living in your home. Perhaps the call would be less painful coming from you or Reverend Rowlands. Would he consider making a personal call on the family?"

Brianna nodded stiffly. "Yes. I just phoned my father. He's on his way over."

But how could she tell the doctor that she had no idea how to contact Marnie's relatives? Marnie had refused to confide any pertinent information about her family's whereabouts. Bree wasn't even sure Smith was Marnie's real last name.

Bree should have made it a point to learn more. She would have to go home now and search Marnie's room for clues to her family background—a driver's license or an address book, perhaps. Surely there would be a clue among Marnie's things.

Within the hour Brianna's father arrived, talked briefly with the doctor, then drove Bree home. Neither of them spoke until her father pulled into the driveway. He stopped the car, swiveled in his seat and gave her his most benevolent smile.

"Honey, I'll go with you to break the news to Marnie's parents. I don't want you facing them alone."

Fresh tears flooded her eyes. "Thanks, Daddy, but first we've got to find them."

Once inside the house, Bree went directly to Marnie's room and began her search, riffling through her closet and drawers. A wave of nausea attacked as she touched Marnie's familiar garments, her toiletries and cosmetics, her personal possessions. There wasn't much to go on. Marnie had arrived with virtually nothing and had accumulated few belongings during her two-month stay. A Bible, a few books and favorite CDs. And, of course, the dog-eared photograph of her handsome brother, Eric, smiling that special smile of his. Brianna winced.

Wherever Eric was, he had no idea he had just lost his sister.

As Bree blinked back a fresh stream of tears, she noticed Marnie's backpack lying beside the bureau. Marnie had forgotten it in their haste to get to the hospital last night. Tentatively Brianna picked it up and opened it—the simple brown canvas bag that still had the feel of Marnie about it. Amid the tissues and toiletries, Bree found a wallet and opened it with awkward fingers, fighting a twinge of guilt. She had worked so hard to build Marnie's trust, and now she was trespassing, invading Marnie's private world. What if Marnie walked in and caught her? She would feel wounded, betrayed. But no, Marnie couldn't walk in. Marnie was…gone.

That was the grim reality that would take ages to accept.

Seizing Marnie's driver's license, Brianna anxiously scanned the name and address. Just as she had suspected, Marnie's last name wasn't Smith. The license read Marnie Wingate and listed a Solana Beach address. Bree flipped through the wallet, looking for additional clues. There were several creased photographs…smiling strangers…people who must have known and loved Marnie…friends…relatives. A distinguished older couple, surely Marnie's parents. Also, several more photos of her brother (even better looking than in the faded snapshot). And one exceptional color portrait of Marnie and Eric when they were children: he stood as tall as a little soldier, the proud older brother with his arm protectively around his baby sister.

If only he could have protected her this time!

And there was a business card. It read: Eric Wingate, Attorney-at-Law, and also listed a Solana Beach address. She turned the card over in her hand, then gazed again at Eric's photographs spread over the bureau. *So this is the man with whom I've felt such a strong emotional connection these past few weeks—the man I've fallen in love with in my fantasies!*

I've got to see Eric first, Bree decided. *I'll break the news to him, and then together we'll tell his parents.*

Brianna quickly showered, applied a touch of makeup and changed into a sedate pantsuit, a pale charcoal gray, as bleak as the news she was delivering. She ran a brush through her long straight hair, then twisted it into an austere chignon. She was the bearer of bad news and might as well look the part.

On her way out the door, her father stopped her and enquired where she was going at a time like this. She told him, and shook her head when he again offered to drive her. "No, Daddy, I've got to do this myself. Marnie was my friend. Her family deserves to hear the news from me, not from some anonymous voice from the hospital, and not even from you."

"I'm not saying you can't go and break the news yourself," he protested. "Just let me drive you, honey."

"No, Daddy. I've got to keep busy and keep my mind off Marnie. I'll feel better driving myself."

She wasn't even sure that was the truth; she just knew she had to carry out this mission alone. Having her father drive her would make her feel like a little girl again, too soft and helpless. She was going to need all the grit and courage she could summon to face Marnie's family.

It took her less than a half-hour to drive to the oceanfront business plaza where Eric Wingate had his office. It was a modern three-story complex of stucco and brick, with a red tile roof and expansive floor-to-ceiling tinted windows. Flanking the parking area was a manicured lawn studded with graceful palm trees and colorful flower boxes. An appealing place to work.

Brianna entered the lobby and found the appropriate office at the end of the hall on the second floor. The sign on the door read, CRAWFORD, WINGATE AND ASSOCIATES. So Eric was already a partner in the company—a successful man by anyone's standards.

She entered gingerly, her breath catching, heart pounding. What would this man be like that she had met only in her dreams and forged solely in her imagination? How could she break this terrible news to him? What could she say to ease his grief?

"May I help you?" asked the receptionist, a sophisticated woman in her late twenties. Bree's face warmed with embarrassment as she realized she had been standing there for several moments lost in thought. "I'd like to see Mr. Wingate."

"Do you have an appointment?"

"No, but I need to speak to him. It's very important."

The receptionist looked at her appointment book. "I can schedule you for tomorrow at nine-thirty."

"No, you don't understand," Bree rushed on miserably. "I've got to see him now. It's a...a personal matter."

The receptionist was obviously well-trained in screening clients and fending off peddlers and solicitors. "What did you say your name was?"

"Brianna Rowlands. But he doesn't know me. Please, I have some important information for him."

"I'm sorry, Miss Rowlands, but whatever you're selling—"

"I'm not selling anything!" Bree exclaimed, too loudly.

An office door opened suddenly, and a tall young man in a three-piece suit stepped out and flashed a quizzical glance.

Eric Wingate! She would know him anywhere! The same riveting eyes and sculpted features that she had memorized from Marnie's photographs.

"Is there a problem, Natalie?"

"No, Mr. Wingate. This lady wants to see you, but she doesn't have an appointment."

As Eric Wingate turned his gaze on Brianna, she felt her knees weaken. She reached out for the corner of the desk. Eric Wingate was far more than his photographs. Easily the handsomest, most imposing man she had ever seen. With the tanned, ruddy glow of a California surfer, he looked as if he had stepped from the pages of a sports magazine. Yet intelligence and sensitivity were etched in his strong masculine features...a solid jaw, patrician nose, and dark brows crouching over intense mahogany-brown eyes. His thick dark hair was stylishly cut, but looked tousled, as if he had a habit of raking his fingers through it while perusing a contract or brief.

"You want to see me?" he enquired in a deep, resonant voice.

"Yes, Mr. Wingate, I do. I...I'm Brianna Rowlands." Still clutching the edge of the desk, she felt light-headed, woozy. The room was warm and the events of the day were catching up with her. When had she last eaten? She couldn't recall. Was it really just this morning that she had lost her cherished friend?

Brianna's knees buckled.

In that instant Eric Wingate sprang forward and caught her in his arms. "Hold my next appointment, Natalie." Masterfully he swept her up, holding her against his solid chest, and carried her into his office.

He eased her gently into a plush leather chair and brought her a cup of cold water from the water cooler. She drank haltingly, on the verge of tears and fighting waves of shame and dread. She wasn't handling this situation well at all. Instead of approaching Eric Wingate from a position of dignity and poise, she had collapsed at his feet in a pitiful bundle of nerves. She had never felt more vulnerable or exposed.

Eric presented her with his monogrammed handkerchief, then sat down at his immense mahogany desk. He didn't take his eyes off her. "How can I help you, Miss Rowlands?" he asked with genuine concern.

"You can't help me," she said, blotting her eyes with the linen handkerchief. "This isn't...it's not about me."

He sat forward and tented his sturdy fingers, his gaze more piercing than ever. "Why don't you tell me what this is about."

"It's Marnie," she managed to say at last.

His eyebrows shot up. "Marnie?"

"Your sister."

He frowned. "My sister is in Europe studying."

Bree swallowed a sob. "No...I'm afraid she's not."

"Of course, she is. I got a postcard from her last week."

"She wanted you to think she was in Europe, but she's been right here in California all summer."

Eric's dark eyes narrowed. "That's impossible. You must have my sister confused with someone else."

"No, Mr. Wingate. There's no mistake. I'm sorry."

"Sorry? Why? What's going on here?"

She blotted her eyes again. "I'm handling this badly. I...I have some bad news for you. I wanted to tell you myself. I didn't want it coming from strangers, although

I realize I...I'm a stranger, too...." She let her voice drift off.

It dawned on her that she was memorizing his face, the glint of bafflement in his eyes, the curve of his lips, the rugged cut of his chin. In a moment everything would change and he would never be the same again. She held that power in her hands—to turn his life upside down with her words. *Dear God, help me! I don't want to do this. Don't make me say the words that could destroy this man!*

His brows lowered, shadowing his eyes. "What on earth are you talking about, Miss Rowlands? Bad news? What news?"

"Your sister...Marnie...she died this morning." There, the words were out! In little more than a whisper.

Eric's face blanched, and he sat back as if he'd been struck. A tendon throbbed along his jaw. After a moment he rallied and leaned across his desk, eyeing her with a steely intensity that made her flinch. "Who are you? What do you want?"

"Nothing," she said quickly. "I didn't want to do this. But you need to know what happened. And how sorry I am."

Eric stood up and crossed the room to the window. He forked his fingers through his thick hair. "Why should I believe you? What do you have to do with my sister?"

Slowly, brokenly, Brianna poured out the entire story, the words jumbled, awkward on her lips, mingled with tears.

After she had finished, Eric stared at her for what seemed forever, his gaze searing her to the bone. "You're telling me my sister was pregnant and had a baby?'' he said through clenched teeth. ''You're saying she died in childbirth? This morning?''

Brianna nodded, fresh tears flowing.

Eric slammed his fist on the desk, startling her from her chair and sending a dozen papers fluttering in the air. ''I've never heard anything so outrageous! If you think you can just walk in here and start spouting outrageous lies about my sister...I don't believe you for a moment!''

With trembling fingers Bree handed him a slip of paper. ''Here's the hospital's phone number. Ask for Dr. Packard in Obstetrics.''

Eric snatched the paper and dialed the number, his lips tight, his jaw clenched, his dubious eyes challenging the veracity of her words. After a minute, he swung his chair around to the window, his back to Brianna, and spoke quietly into the receiver. Gradually his voice grew louder and more animated, broken finally by a deep, guttural sob, and then long moments of silence as he struggled to compose himself.

Bree looked away, feeling like an intruder, even though she couldn't see his face, could detect his despair only in his drooping shoulders and bowed head. Finally he wheeled back around to his desk and dropped the receiver into its cradle. As if he had forgotten she was there, he put his head in his hands and sobbed convulsively, his shoulders heaving, the sounds erupting raw and ragged and deep.

Bree watched with growing misgivings. She wanted to get up and run out the door; she also wanted to rush to this grieving man, wrap her arms around him and comfort him. She did neither. She waited with growing mortification until Eric Wingate choked back his sobs and struggled to compose himself. She considered offering him the handkerchief he had given her, then dismissed the idea and sighed with relief when he produced a box of tissues from his desk drawer.

"I apologize, Miss Rowlands," he said as he dried his reddened eyes. "Believe me, I'm not one to display my emotions before strangers, but your news hit me hard. I loved my sister very much."

"And she loved you. She spoke of you with great devotion."

"Did she?"

Brianna could see Eric sloughing off his grief like a restrictive cloak and becoming the quintessential lawyer once again. He methodically rubbed his chin and gazed off into space as if mentally putting together pieces of a puzzle. At last he looked at her, every vestige of emotion sealed behind his professional facade.

"Miss Rowlands, you said my sister was living at your home?"

She nodded and repeated the explanation as to how Marnie had come to live with her family. "She became like a sister to me, and I think she felt the same way. We were very close."

Eric straightened a stack of papers on his desk. "Then why, Miss Rowlands, didn't you encourage my sister to contact her family? Why didn't you urge her to go home where she belonged?"

Brianna stiffened, her voice coming out wooden and defensive. "I did suggest that, Mr. Wingate, but Marnie was adamant about not letting her family know she was pregnant. She planned to return home in the fall, after her baby was born and adopted by a good family."

Eric shoved back his chair and stood abruptly. He paced back and forth, pummeling his palm with his fist. "So Marnie was going to go on as if nothing had happened? She was going to pretend she had been in Europe all summer? I can't imagine Marnie doing that.'' He stared at Brianna. ''Why would she do such a thing, Miss Rowlands? Why would she shut her family out of her life just when she needed us most?''

Brianna groped for words. ''She…she didn't want to disappoint you, or your parents. Especially your parents. She was convinced they would never forgive her. She was ready to do anything to keep from hurting them.''

''Hurting them? Are you kidding? This will kill them!'' Eric took longer strides, pacing the room, moving with a nervous agitation as if empowered by an energy beyond himself. ''I can't make sense of it. I can't understand how she could turn from us at a time like this. How she could rob us of the chance to help and support her. I took care of her all of our lives, watched out for her, protected her the way a big brother should.'' He paused and looked sharply at Brianna. ''It infuriates me…devastates me, that I wasn't there for her.''

Tears welled in Brianna's eyes. ''I wish it could have been different. I'm so sorry.''

Eric Wingate approached her as if circling an enemy, his piercing eyes fastened on her. ''You say you're a counselor, Miss Wingate. Then, why didn't you convince my sister to go home? You're older and wiser, I assume. A professional woman, trained in these matters. Why did you let her live a lie?''

All Brianna's defenses dissolved under Eric Wingate's searing scrutiny. ''I…I tried to tell her, but she wouldn't listen.'' Bree's throat tightened. Her tongue felt thick, dry. Nothing she said could make a difference to this man. Nothing! He was struggling to comprehend one of the worst losses of his life, and he obviously held Brianna responsible. "Marnie was a grown woman," she said, her voice riding on a fresh wave of tears. "She had made up her mind. What could I do? I...I never even knew her real identity until today."

At the sight of Brianna's tears, Eric Wingate seemed to mellow. He ambled over, placed an awkward hand on her shoulder and said solemnly, "It's too late for recriminations and guilt. We have other things to think about now. The baby. And how to tell my parents that Marnie is gone."

Bree looked up at him. "I'll help you if you want. I'll go with you to tell them."

He nodded. "They'll want to know everything... things only you would know—about Marnie's state of mind, her pregnancy, her baby."

"I'll tell them everything I can."

Eric sat down on the edge of his desk. His voice rumbled with emotion. "You say the baby's okay? Healthy? Ten fingers, ten toes, all of that good stuff?"

"Yes, she's beautiful. Small, of course. Born a month early. They have her in an incubator to help with her breathing. But, barring any complications, the pediatrician thinks she'll be able to go home in a few days."

"Home?"

"Yes. Home. With me." Bree realized the word had raised a red flag. What if Eric and his parents didn't agree with Marnie's wishes? "You see, Marnie asked me to take the baby...she made me temporary guardian. She wanted me to find a good home for her little girl. I said I would."

"You mean adopt the child out? Give her away?"

Bree felt herself recoiling under Eric's scathing gaze. She forced out the words. "It's what Marnie wanted."

"What about her family?" Eric shot back. "Don't we have a say?"

Bree weighed her words carefully. "Marnie didn't think her family would want to raise an infant. Your parents are older and not in the best of health, and you're a single man with a demanding career."

Eric expelled a sharp breath. Some of his wrath seemed to dissolve, as well. "Okay, maybe she's right. But she didn't give us a chance to say no, did she."

Something in Eric's expression—a flash of wounded, boyish vulnerability—struck at the core of Brianna's heart. She wanted to embrace this man she had known only in her imagination for so many weeks. Wanted to comfort him. And, as incredible as it seemed, *love him.*

She closed her eyes, shutting him out. For crying out loud, was she coming totally unglued? What was wrong with her, thinking of loving a stranger? She forced her mind back to the subject at hand, but her face and throat felt uncomfortably warm.

"No, Mr. Wingate," she said quietly, steadying her voice. "I'm sorry that your sister didn't consult you or your parents about your wishes. But she did what she thought was the best thing for her baby."

"And she was dead wrong!" Dark fires flamed in Eric's eyes. He inhaled deeply, and as the air filled his lungs he seemed to grow even taller and more imposing. He crossed his brawny arms on his broad chest and spoke with a flinty edge in his voice. "We could talk in circles all day, Miss Rowlands, and it wouldn't bring Marnie back. Right now we need to go…break the news to my parents. Are you ready?"

Bree nodded, but already she felt like a tiny craft that had been battered at sea by gales of wind and torrents of rain. Somehow she had found the fortitude to confront Eric Wingate with the tragic news of his sister's death. But she wasn't sure she could summon the strength to face his parents, as well.

She knew only one thing at this fateful moment. God help her, she didn't want to let the inscrutable and disarming Eric Wingate out of her sight...or out of her life.

Chapter Six

"Thanks, Juliana, for coming with me today. You're a lifesaver!" Andrew Rowlands was holding Juliana's slim hand, his fingers intertwined with hers as they strolled along a grassy cliff overlooking a bejeweled, teal-blue ocean at La Jolla Cove, one of Andrew's favorite places. He had come here often after Mandy's death to gaze at the ocean and talk with God. Now he wanted to build fresh memories here with Juliana, even if he wasn't sure what those memories would be.

He looked down at her and winked. "Jewel, this outing is just what the doctor ordered."

She gave a musical little laugh. "For me, too, Andrew. The perfect prescription for a perfect day." Juliana's strawberry-red lips caressed each word as a playful breeze teased her long, raven tresses, sending silky ringlets over her forehead and along her high cheekbones. Her flaming orange sundress accentuated her sun-bronzed skin as she gazed up at him with adoring, smoky-brown eyes. She had never looked more beautiful.

Was that ardor in her expression or did he see only the reflection of his own long-suppressed desire? All day he had yearned to gather her into his arms and smother her with kisses...to hold her and feel the warmth of her against his chest. The intensity of his emotions startled and unnerved him. Where was all this volatile, unbidden sentiment coming from?

You're a dignified minister of God, Rowlands, old man! Watch what you're thinking! But he was a flesh-and-blood man, as well, and it had been years now since he had truly loved a woman, body and soul.

But he dare not think of that now. He had vowed that he and Juliana would remain friends. Just friends.

They had reached a small gazebo at the edge of the bluff overlooking sandy beaches and rocky promonto-ries. The view was magnificent. Fleecy clouds scudded along a cerulean skyline. Whitecaps rolled in, crashing over the jagged shoals while the sun caught the glitter of diamonds on the spangled sea.

Andrew leaned one arm on the railing and circled Juliana's narrow waist with his free arm. "So what do you think of my secret hideaway?"

"Oh, Andrew, it is breathtaking."

"Yes, it is, isn't it." But he was looking at Juliana now, not the scenery. She was so full of life and vitality. He needed that now, a breath of fresh air, the sensation of feeling keenly, joyously alive.

Juliana looked up and laughed in delight. "Andrew, look! A pelican flying right over us. Almost close enough to touch."

He grinned and pointed to a grassy crag nearby. "And there, in the grass, a family of squirrels."

"Oh, I love it here, Andrew. Listen to the seagulls calling to one another. They love it, too."

Andrew breathed in the clean, moist air, pungent with salt spray. He always felt invigorated when he came to this spot. But today he felt something more, an emotion he had no words for. It was pleasant and bittersweet all at once.

Juliana nestled her head against his chest. "You seem in such a mood today, Andrew. Wistful...sad...quiet."

He inhaled sharply. "It's been quite a week, Juliana. I think I'm just beginning to feel the effects of it all."

She slipped her hand over his. "No wonder, dear heart. This past week you have been so strong and brave and caring to so many. You saw me through my daughter's reconstructive surgery. You conducted a beautiful funeral service for our poor Marnie. You gave comfort to your daughter and the entire Wingate family. You have given out so much. Now you need someone to give to you."

"You've given a lot, too, dear Jewel," Andrew noted softly. "You arranged that wonderful dinner after the funeral. You were a most gracious hostess—the way you went around welcoming everyone, and comforting and affirming them and making them feel at ease. You made the day easier for all of us with your warmth and generosity. You make people feel you really care."

"Because I do. I love people. I love helping them. I have lived with pain, too...my husband's death in the car crash and Belina's paralysis and lengthy recuperation. Helping hurting people brings me joy."

"It shows. You have a way of touching their hearts, making them laugh, giving them hope."

"Not unlike what you do, Andrew."

He nuzzled the top of her head. "Guess we make quite a team, huh?"

"I've thought that for some time," she murmured. "You are such a dear friend."

I want to be so much more, he mused silently. But he still wasn't sure whether he was responding to his own desires or God's will. If he gave in recklessly to his impulses, he would only be hurting Juliana...and himself. Best to wait on God's timing.

Juliana had already moved on to another subject. "Have you heard from the Wingate family since the funeral?"

"Not a word. As far as Brianna knows, they haven't even gone to the hospital to see the baby."

Juliana shook her head solemnly. "Marnie's parents...such peculiar people. At the funeral, their faces were like stone. No sign of grief, and yet they had to be in such pain. Now, we Italians...we let the world know when we are hurting!"

"But it's not just their stoicism that bothers me. It's their attitude toward the baby. You would think they'd want to see their grandchild, especially after losing their daughter."

"Maybe they blame the baby for Marnie's death."

Andrew nodded. "I suppose they're in denial. If they don't see the baby, they don't have to deal with losing their daughter. Maybe they've blocked from their minds the reason for her death."

"I'm glad they chose you to officiate at her funeral."

"That was her brother's doing. He felt it was what Marnie would have wanted, especially since his parents have no church home."

"You gave a wonderful message, Andrew. "You let everyone know that Marnie came to love the Lord and was happy and at peace when she died."

"Yes, we can be thankful for that." He paused and

gazed out at the reddening skyline. Daylight was already slipping away. How quickly the hours fled. Especially when he was with his precious Juliana. "By the way," he said, nuzzling her hair again, "the baby will be released from the hospital tomorrow."

She stirred in his arms. "I didn't know."

"Brianna will be bringing little Charity home until she can find a suitable couple to adopt her."

"I think Bree has already become attached to the child."

"She would love to keep the baby, but our household isn't set up to raise a newborn, with all of us working and keeping such long hours. Bree knows the baby needs a real family, both a mother and father who can devote themselves to her."

"But after losing Marnie, Bree may find it hard to let the child go. She may be surprised by the depth of her feelings."

"I'm sure that's true," Andrew conceded. "She and Marnie were like sisters."

"And if I'm not mistaken, Marnie had become like a daughter to you."

Andrew flinched in spite of himself. He felt his mouth grow dry and a sour taste rise at the back of his throat. "Yes, she was like a daughter. I'd grown very fond of her. The house…it feels incredibly empty now. There's a pall over everything. It's almost like…like…"

Juliana said the words he couldn't articulate. "Like when Mandy died?"

"How did you know?"

"Because I know what grief feels like and smells like and tastes like. Grief is a formidable enemy. It doesn't give up its stranglehold easily. A new loss always sends you back to the old one."

"Exactly." Andrew released Juliana and absently rubbed his jaw as he gazed at the darkening skyline. "I feel as if I've lost Mandy all over again. But I can't bear to retrace all those agonizing steps. I don't want my home to be a house of mourning. I want it to be a house of joy. I want to be a man of joy again. Is that selfish? Too much to ask?"

Juliana gazed up at him with wide, glistening eyes. "No, Andrew. You deserve to be happy again. It's time to move on."

"I thought I had. I thought I'd already covered this ground and grieved past this point. I thought I was over this, and yet it's all come back, like a flood, like those waves down there, washing in over the sand and receding. And just when I think they're gone, they wash in again even harder, nearly toppling me emotionally with their force."

She twined her arm in his. "I'm sorry, Andrew. I wish I knew how to help."

"You are helping. Just by listening."

"Then go on. Tell me how you feel."

He shrugged. "Right now, I just want the waves to wash away all the hurt. I'm tired of grieving. It's as if I'm stuck in neutral, or reverse, when all I want to do is plow through the pain to something else. I want to feel life pulsing in me again—joyous, exuberant life. I want to laugh without feeling guilty. I want to love again, in every way." His voice grew husky. "And yet I realize I may never have that right. It may not be in God's plan for me to marry again."

Juliana tightened her hold on his arm. "But perhaps it is God's will and you have missed His signals, Andrew. Perhaps fear keeps both of us from reaching out for someone to love."

Her words had the absolute ring of truth. Instinctively Andrew drew Juliana into his arms and searched her bright, mahogany eyes. "What a tragic shame if fear has kept us apart."

Juliana parted her lips, as if to speak, but he silenced her with a kiss filled with exquisite tenderness. She responded freely. Andrew felt dizzy, light-headed, as if fireworks were going off in his head.

It took every ounce of willpower to draw back and release her, although his arms remained loosely around her waist. "What am I going to do with you?" he asked as he traced the heart-shaped line of her pursed lips.

"I don't know, Andrew," she answered. "What do you want to do?"

"Love you," he said simply, honestly. "You dazzle me, mystify me, leave me delirious and defenseless. The truth is, I absolutely adore you, Juliana Pagliarulo. I can't imagine myself living without you."

Juliana's smile was radiant. "And I feel the same way about you, Andrew. You make me feel like a lovesick teenager again." Her voice took on a wistful note. "But, of course, we are not teenagers."

"No, far from it. We're adults with very separate lives and commitments."

"So what do we do with this love blossoming in our hearts?" she challenged. "Deny it? Pray for it to go away?"

"I don't know, Juliana. A part of me wants to make you my bride and whisk you away to some enchanted castle just for the two of us. But another part of me realizes that to make you my bride would be to change your life drastically, in ways you couldn't possibly be prepared for."

"You mean, by marrying you, I would become a minister's wife," she murmured thoughtfully.

"Yes, and I believe no woman should accept that role unless God has called her to it. It's not an easy life."

"But rewarding, I'm sure."

"Extremely rewarding."

Her eyes twinkled with a demure spark. "Then perhaps it is something I should pray about."

Andrew gently wound one of her ebony curls around his index finger. "My dear Juliana, are you saying...?"

A coquettish smile played on her glossy red lips. "Yes, Andrew. I am."

He drew her against him, and she nestled her head against his chest. Was it possible? This magnificent woman would consider blending her life with his and making his calling her own?

His voice broke with rising emotion. "If you're willing to consider becoming a minister's wife...*my* wife, then by all means we should pray about it. Both of us. Together. Beginning right now...before the sun sets on another day."

Chapter Seven

The phone was ringing off the hook. Brianna was already late, dashing out the door, riding on adrenaline, heading for the hospital to pick up baby Charity. So let someone else answer the phone. "Is anybody going to get that?" she shouted from the doorway. It was probably a parishioner, or a pushy solicitor wanting them to change their phone service.

No doubt her father was in his study and Frannie was in the sunroom working on her latest sculpture. So all right, she'd get it. She set her purse and brand-new diaper bag on the floor and crossed the room in quick strides. She grabbed up the receiver and breathlessly barked, "Hello!"

"Miss Rowlands?" The deep masculine voice was faintly, pleasantly familiar.

"Yes, this is she."

"This is Eric Wingate."

Brianna's knees turned to gelatin and her heart caught in her throat. "Oh, yes, Mr. Wingate. I'm sorry, I was just on my way out the door."

"I won't keep you, Miss Rowlands. I just wondered...I understand you're bringing Marnie's baby home today."

"Yes, that's where I'm going now. To the hospital. Is there a problem?"

"No, not at all. I think it's quite generous of you to do this for my sister, to take care of the child until you find her a good home."

"It's not generous at all, Mr. Wingate. I want to do it." Brianna forced her voice to remain calm. Why did this man—still a virtual stranger—have this effect on her, prompting a panic attack every time she heard his voice or saw his face? All because she had allowed herself to fantasize over his photograph—a worn snapshot Marnie had carried like a secret treasure in her bib overalls. "Like I told you at the funeral, Mr. Wingate, I promised Marnie I would find Charity a loving home. And I won't rest until I've done that."

"I'm sure you won't. Marnie was fortunate to have you for a friend, Miss Rowlands. But I thought perhaps you would like some assistance. I am an attorney and I have handled a number of adoptions. Perhaps together we could make sure my sister's last wishes are fulfilled."

"That's kind of you, Mr. Wingate." Bree's heart rate was soaring. The idea of working with this man in any manner raised goose bumps on her arms. "I suppose I will need an attorney to make arrangements for the adoption. Frankly, I'm not even sure where to start."

"Then, I trust you won't mind my help. I know you'll be busy taking care of the baby for the next few days. I could come there if you like. And I should see her...I mean, I hate to admit this, but I haven't even seen the baby yet." His voice caught on a wave of unexpected emotion. "I've put it off, and I shouldn't have. My parents didn't want to go to the hospital. But it's time. I need to see my sister's baby."

"Of course, Mr. Wingate. Come over anytime."

"This evening, perhaps?"

She struggled to find her voice. "All right, yes, if you like. I have no idea what to expect. It'll be the baby's first night home. I mean, here, at my home."

"Then, maybe you'll need an extra pair of hands." He chuckled ruefully. "Not that I know the first thing about babies."

"That's all right. I don't know a thing, either. But I'm sure I can use all the help I can get."

"Fine. I'll be there about seven?"

"Seven would be fine."

But seven was anything but fine. By the time Eric Wingate arrived at the Rowlands' home, Brianna was fit to be tied. She had already spent the past three hours walking the floor with little Charity. No matter what Bree tried, the baby would not be comforted. Now, as Bree led Eric into the family room while bouncing Charity on her shoulder, the swaddled infant's cry rose to an ear-splitting shriek.

"Yes, she's a Wingate, all right," Eric acknowledged. "I'd recognize that squall anywhere." He folded back the pastel-pink receiving blanket and smiled grimly at Charity's tiny beet-red face. "She's got Marnie's eyes."

"She's beautiful, isn't she?" murmured Brianna. "But I'm frazzled. I can't seem to make her happy. I must be doing something wrong."

"I doubt it. Babies are supposed to cry, aren't they?"

"I suppose, but she's been crying for three hours."

"You fed her?"

"Yes. Two bottles of formula. She can't still be hungry, can she?"

Eric shrugged. "I haven't the faintest idea." He ran his knuckles lightly over the baby's pink cheek. "At least her cry seems to be striking a lower decibel level than before."

As if on cue, little Charity stiffened her body and let out a howl that startled them both.

"Is your family here?" questioned Eric, looking around. "I think we need to bring in reinforcements."

Bree shook her head. Over Charity's caterwauls, she shouted, "My father's at a deacon's meeting and my sister is teaching an evening art class at San Diego State. I'm afraid we're on our own."

Eric gave her a helpless shrug. "Maybe she's just tired. They say babies sleep a lot."

"Good thought," said Bree. "I'll try putting her in her crib. Um, would you like to see the nursery?"

"Sure. Lead the way."

Cradling a wailing Charity in her arms, Bree led Eric upstairs to the third room on the left. This had once been her mother's sewing room. Now it was a makeshift nursery, complete with a crib, changing table, playpen and high chair. Brianna gently laid Charity in the crib, which prompted the infant to wail all the louder.

"Do you think she's okay?" Eric enquired worriedly. "Her face is as red as a tomato."

Bree shrugged. Panic was setting in. She must be doing something wrong. At this rate she would surely earn the title Worst Stand-in Mother of the Year. "Maybe I should call the doctor."

"First, let me try my hand at this." Eric slipped off his tan sport jacket, removed his gold cuff links, and rolled up his sleeves. Gingerly he scooped up Charity in his arms and held her against his shoulder. "Did you burp her?"

"Yes, I tried. I patted her after each bottle, but I didn't hear a burp. I was afraid to pat her too hard. She's so tiny and fragile."

"Let me see what I can do." Eric paced the floor, rhythmically thumping Charity's back.

Suddenly Brianna heard a loud belch. "Was that the baby?"

"It wasn't me," retorted Eric, sounding mildly annoyed.

Bree's face grew warm. "I didn't mean to imply—"

"Oh, for crying out loud!" Eric sprang forward and quickly handed the baby back to Brianna.

She stared at him in confusion. "What's wrong?"

Eric rubbed his hands over his shirtfront. With his dark hair curling over his forehead and his face scrunched in a frown, he looked like a peeved, vulnerable little boy. He twisted his mouth in disgust and muttered, "Baby spit-up!"

Bree stifled a chuckle. "At least Charity is happy now. Look— She stopped crying. You must have that magic touch."

"She's just pleased with herself for ruining my best shirt."

Brianna laid the baby gently in her crib and tucked her pink flannel blanket around her. Charity's eyes were already closed, and she was making contented little sucking sounds with her rosebud lips.

With one last glance at her slumbering charge, Brianna turned to Eric to assess the damage to his dress shirt. "That can be washed out," she informed him.

"Meanwhile, I'm going to smell like sour milk."

"No, we can fix it now. Just give me your shirt."

A mischievous gleam shone in his dark eyes. "Give you my shirt? You want the shirt off my back?"

She smiled patiently. "Unless you want me to wash it with you in it."

Eric promptly unbuttoned his shirt and shrugged out of it, revealing a tanned, powerful chest and muscular arms. For a moment Bree forgot the baby spit-up and simply gazed approvingly at the exquisite Eric Wingate.

Eric handed her the shirt. "I will get it back tonight, won't I? If the cops stop me, I'll have a time explaining how I lost my shirt."

"You'll have it back in an hour. I'll just wash it and toss it in the dryer." She put her finger to her lips. "Let's see if we can sneak downstairs without waking the baby."

They were halfway down the stairs, Eric bare-chested and Brianna carrying his shirt, when they encountered her father just starting up the stairs. It was an awkward moment for everyone.

"Daddy, you remember Eric Wingate…"

"Of course. Good to see you again, Eric. Did you, uh, have an accident? Spill some food?"

"No, it's…actually it's baby spit-up. Your daughter offered to wash my shirt."

"Oh, well, carry on, then. Good to see you again. Give your parents my regards."

"I will, sir."

Brianna stole off to the laundry room, while Eric made himself comfortable in the family room, flipping through a business magazine. When she returned, he was putting on his sport coat over his bare chest. She sat down on the love seat across from him. "It shouldn't take long. About an hour."

"Then, while we're waiting, I suppose we can talk about Charity. Our options. Her future."

"Okay. What do you have in mind?"

"I brought some names of clients with me, couples who are desperate to adopt a baby. Maybe we can find Charity's family from among them."

"I'd want to meet them first."

"That's the idea. That's what Marnie wanted. You can pick out the most likely candidates from the profiles I've brought with me, and I'll set up interviews with the potential clients. Of course, I'll have someone in the firm handle the legal process, to avoid any conflict of interest."

"Are you saying I can sit in on the interviews?"

"Of course. You're Charity's temporary guardian. Marnie would want you to approve of the family that raises her."

"Then, I guess we should start by reading over the profiles." She hesitated. "Do you have time tonight?"

He flashed an easy smile. "Sure. Nothing waiting for me at my apartment except more work. Let me get my briefcase out of the car. I'll be right back."

"And I'll go put some coffee on. Um, you do like coffee, don't you?"

"Sure do. Strong, with just a hint of cream."

"Great. I may even scrounge up some of my sister's fresh-baked cookies."

His smile deepened. "Sounds good. I'll hurry."

Eric left and returned moments later, striding tall with his briefcase in hand, looking every ounce the professional—except where his bare chest showed disarmingly through his open jacket. Bree showed him to the kitchen, where he spread the paperwork over the oak table; she set out a plate of cookies and two china cups and saucers. For the next two hours they sipped their cups of steaming hot coffee, munched chocolate chip cookies, and pored over a dozen adoption applications.

At last Brianna sat back and shook her head. "This is so hard. Every couple sounds deserving, and desperate for a baby."

Eric nodded. "They are both deserving and desperate. You encounter a lot of needy people in this business. Couples who have tried for years to have children, and it never happens for them. Some couples have one child but want a larger family. They don't want to raise an only child. Some couples have lost a child and think another child will ease their emptiness."

Brianna sat forward with her elbows on the table. "So how do we decide who gets Charity?"

Eric drummed his fingers on the stack of applications. "Pray about it, I suppose. At least, that's what I do when I face difficult decisions."

Bree smiled. "I'm impressed, Mr. Wingate. I didn't expect a practical, analytical attorney to be a praying man."

He chuckled. "I wasn't always. And believe me, it's not the way I was raised. My parents wanted nothing to do with religion. But a few years ago a colleague invited me to his church. I was skeptical, but I went, anyway, figuring I could shoot the pastor's message full of holes. But instead of being confronted with a dry, dusty theology I could argue with, I came face-to-face with the Person of Christ. I couldn't argue away His love. When I realized God was offering me a relationship with Him and not just a rigid set of rules, I gave Him my life. It was the least I could do. His Son had given His life for me."

Bree nodded, a pleasant warmth spreading across her

cheeks and down her throat. So Eric Wingate was a believer! One more reason for this odd, unspoken bond she felt with him. "I feel the same way, Mr. Wingate. My walk with Christ is very precious to me. But I must admit—"

"Eric, please. Call me Eric."

The warmth in her face deepened. "If you'll call me Bree."

His eyes crinkled at the corners. "Bree, it is. And you were saying?"

"Nothing really. It's just…being raised in the church, sometimes I'm afraid I take my faith for granted."

"I suppose that's easy to do when you've never experienced the dark side of life. You don't realize how bad it can be out there without the Lord."

Bree traced the rim of her china cup with one long polished nail. "I caught a fresh glimpse of God's love and power when your sister came to faith in Christ. Her whole personality and demeanor changed. It was beautiful."

Eric's expression shifted slightly, as if he were warding off an expected blow. He focused his attention on his coffee, his brows knit in a frown as he turned the delicate cup between his large palms. "I'm thankful you were able to help her," he murmured, his voice erupting in a low rumble, like the gritty vibration of a truck on a bumpy road. "I didn't know how to reach her. We were close once, but lately she was so distant, so remote. I kept thinking I must have done something…"

"It wasn't you, Eric. She just didn't want you to know she was pregnant."

He lowered his gaze, the shadow of his dark lashes feathering his ruddy cheeks. He pinched the bridge of his nose and made a strangled sound low in his throat, as if to keep back a sob. "I...I can't believe she's gone."

Brianna reached across the table and patted his hand. Eric had strong, sturdy hands, capable and protective, hands a woman could depend on. Or was that mere wishful thinking—more of Bree's foolish fantasies? "Your sister loved you very much, Eric," she said gently. "She talked about you all the time. You were...her hero."

Eric's countenance darkened and his eyes flashed fire. "Some hero! I couldn't even save her!"

"Don't blame yourself. There was nothing anyone could do. Don't you see? Only God could have saved her."

Eric stared frankly at her. "Then, why didn't He?"

Bree's voice came out small and pained. "I don't know. I asked the same question about my mother. Why would God take her? She was the most godly woman I'd ever known."

"Did you ever come up with an answer, any insight you care to share?"

"Only that we can trust God even when we can't trace Him."

"Yes, I'm familiar with that saying. But, of course, it's easier said than done, isn't it."

Bree smiled ruefully. "Yes, much easier. I fall on my face so many times when it comes to trusting God. Sometimes, especially after my mother died, I just wanted to shout at Him and demand an explanation."

"At least you're honest about your feelings. That's how I feel now about Marnie. But even David and Jeremiah and Job railed against God at times."

"And they always came back to Him, in faith. They knew that if we could understand why God does everything He does, He wouldn't be God. His ways are beyond our ability to understand or predict. And there's one more thing I know for sure."

"What's that?"

"He's a God of vast and incomprehensible love. We can depend on Him to do what's best for us, no matter what."

Eric smiled. "True. No matter what."

"More coffee?" asked Bree, reaching for the coffee-pot.

He waved her off. "No, I'm fine. But, uh, I could use my shirt."

Bree put her hand to her mouth, remembering. "Oh, of course. I'm sorry. I'll be right back." She got up and hurried to the laundry room, retrieved Eric's shirt from the dryer and returned to the kitchen. "Here it is, good as new," she said, shaking out the wrinkles.

As Eric sloughed off his jacket, she politely turned her eyes away, then stole a surreptitious glance. He might be a lawyer with a desk job, but he obviously found time to work out.

He took the shirt, pulled it on and buttoned it, smoothing the creases with his palms. "Still warm from the dryer. Feels good."

She smiled, her cheeks warming again. "We aim to please."

"I have a few dozen more at home," he quipped. "My dry cleaner never delivers them like this."

She chuckled. "Maybe I've discovered a whole new career."

Eric slipped on his jacket with ease, then glanced up at the wall clock. "Well, Brianna, I guess it's time for me to go."

What's your hurry? she wanted to ask, but resisted

the impulse. Already she felt an emptiness inside at the thought of him leaving. There was so much more she wanted to know about him. Just spending these quiet, ordinary moments together made her feel happy and content in a way she'd never felt with any other man. *Stop it, Bree! It's just your overactive imagination! Let the poor man go home!*

Lifting her chin resolutely, she escorted him from the kitchen and fell into step with him as they crossed the living room to the foyer. "Thanks for coming over," she said, as he opened the door.

He paused on the threshold, smiling at her with those eyes. "No, I'm the one who should thank you, Bree. Thanks for letting me see my little niece. Somehow, holding Charity made me feel closer to my sister."

"You're welcome to come again, if you wish."

He nodded. "Maybe I will. I'd like to see the baby again."

"Anytime. Your parents are welcome to come, too."

His expression clouded. "Don't count on it. I think they're in denial. They've half convinced themselves Marnie really is in Europe. Seeing her baby would only bring home the painful reality of it all, and my folks have never been good at handling reality."

Bree touched his arm. "I'm sorry, Eric. That must make it awfully difficult for you."

"It was…while I was still living at home. I got my own place a couple of years ago, a nice little apartment near my office. Of course, I felt like I was deserting Marnie, but I had to get out. Now I only visit my parents after I've worked up the moxie to deal with them."

"Just the same, let them know they can visit the baby."

"They won't, but I will. When would be a good time?"

She shrugged. "Whenever. I was thinking of taking Charity to the park on Saturday. Get her out in the fresh air."

"The little park a couple of blocks from here?"

"Yes. You've seen it?"

"Drove by it on my way here." He squeezed her arm lightly. "Tell you what. Folks accuse me of being all work, no play, but I'm going to break the mold. I'll bring a picnic lunch, and we'll make a real day of it. What do you say?"

Bree felt a schoolgirl grin spread from ear to ear. "Okay. Sure, Eric. Sounds like fun. About noon?"

"Noon it is. What'll it be? Takeout chicken? Deli subs? Chinese? Or honey-baked ham and potato salad?"

She clasped her hands together, already brimming with anticipation. "I don't know. Whatever. Surprise me."

His lips curled into a sly, winsome smile that tugged her heartstrings. "So you're a girl who likes surprises, huh?"

"Sure. Nice ones. Who doesn't?"

"Then, surprised you'll be." He stepped out onto the sprawling porch and gave her a little salute. "Until Saturday."

"Saturday," she echoed in a hushed whisper.

As she closed the door after him, her heart was riding a carousel of joy. She and Eric Wingate would be spending a whole grand and glorious day together! And was she mistaken, or had she seen the same flicker of affection in his eyes that was surely shining in her own?

Maybe dreams came true, after all!

Chapter Eight

꩜

Saturday was a perfect day for a picnic—warm and balmy, with a glorious sun that played hide-and-seek with the scudding clouds. Except for a few joggers and a handful of children on the playground equipment, Eric and Brianna had the park to themselves. The air was redolent of sweet freshly mown grass and tangy honeysuckle.

Brianna had covered the rough-hewn picnic table with a vinyl red-checkered tablecloth, and Eric had set out his basket of goodies including plastic plates and tableware, a bottle of sparkling cider, a cellophane bag of fresh fruit—apples, bananas, grapes and strawberries—and several mysterious cardboard containers.

"I hope you like quesadillas," Eric said as he checked one of the containers. "I tell you, these are out of this world. You haven't eaten until you've tried one. Chock-full of tomatoes, mushrooms, green chiles and guacamole."

Brianna, lazily ensconced on the bench seat beside Charity's infant carrier, clasped her hands in bemused delight. "Oh, Eric, I love Mexican food! How did you guess?"

He gave her a sly grin that actually tickled her tummy. He looked wonderfully appealing in a tank top and cutoff jeans, so unlike the aloof, urbane attorney he had appeared to be in his office two weeks ago.

"I had a feeling," he was saying in that sonorous voice of his. "You look like a fajitas-and-tamales girl to me. Besides, it's my favorite, too. I figured if you didn't like it, I could always buy you a fast-food burger while I polish off these south-of-the-border delicacies."

Bree playfully crossed her arms and jutted out her chin. She was wearing a chambray-blue, button-front romper that showed off her tanned legs and arms. "No way, José! You're looking at the world's champion fajitas eater. Especially if they're loaded with lots of fresh bell peppers and *pico de gallo.*"

"Whoops! I'm afraid we haven't a bell pepper in the house. But I ordered extra cheese and sour cream."

She shrugged. "Okay, I'll manage."

"But no onions."

She laughed. "All the better to keep from offending one another." She stole a veiled glance at him, wondering if he took her remark the wrong way. After all, they weren't likely to get that close to each other, anyway. But he was chuckling, too, with a canny look that said he wouldn't mind a little closeness. Or was that her wishful thinking again?

She baited him with "So are you saying you didn't whip up this little repast with your own two hands?"

"I cannot tell a lie. I used my hands…to dial Diego's Cantina and to pick up my order."

As he opened the largest container, the tantalizing

aroma of chorizo, scallions and jalapeños filled Bree's senses.

She inhaled deeply. "It smells delicious!"

Eric sat down on the opposite bench and distributed the plastic plates and utensils. "Maybe we'd better eat while the baby's sleeping."

Bree nodded emphatically. "I'm still trying to get the hang of this mothering business. Charity kept me up half the night, walking the floor. I tried everything. Rocking her, feeding her, burping her, even singing to her. Nothing helped."

"So what did you do?"

"I finally put her in bed with me, and she went right to sleep, happy as a lark."

A smile played on Eric's lips, as if he were about to say something and thought better of it. He looked away, but not before his beguiling expression made Bree blush. She rushed on, filling the awkward silence with a blitz of words. "But I can't make a habit of letting her sleep with me, can I? I can't let her get attached, thinking I'm her mommy. After all, she won't be with me that long. I'll be using up my vacation time from the counseling center in a few weeks. But by then we'll be finding her a family of her own."

"You bet." Eric opened the rest of the containers— tamales, refried beans, rice, nachos. "So let's say Grace and eat before our little Charity gives a replay of last night."

Bree nodded, and Eric said a simple conversational prayer. For the next few minutes they turned their attention to the food. "Excellent!" Bree sighed when she had finished her quesadilla. "And so much better when you're eating outdoors."

Eric refilled their plastic cups with sparkling cider,

taking care not to spill a drop. "To be honest, I've never been a picnic sort of guy. But yes, it is jolly good fun, now that you mention it."

"Didn't your parents ever take you on a picnic when you were a little boy?"

"Are you kidding? With all the ants and mosquitoes and dirt and grime? No way. Every meal was in the dining room with my mom's best linen, china and silver."

"Formal meals are nice, but there are times when it's fun just to eat pizza and hot dogs on paper plates in the kitchen."

Eric shook his head. "No paper plates in my mother's house. She keeps up appearances even when no one's watching."

Bree traced the checkered pattern on the oilcloth. "I can see why Marnie couldn't tell her mother her problems. Were you and your sister ever allowed to make mistakes?"

"We heard about it when we did. It wasn't the discipline I minded. It was the look of condescension in my mother's eyes."

"That must have been painful."

"More for Marnie than for me. She could never get it right. But me, I learned early to put on a good show for my mother. Get good grades. Mind my manners. Be the perfect little boy she expected. But all the time I was gritting my teeth and loathing my mother for not accepting me as I was. It wasn't until I was an adult that I began to see my mother for the woman she is."

"And what did you see?"

"A rigid, lonely, frustrated woman with the self-esteem of a gnat. She couldn't accept anyone else, not even her husband and children, because she couldn't accept herself. No matter how hard she tried, she couldn't measure up to her own impossible standards.''

''That's quite an insight,'' mused Bree. ''You must be able to read people amazingly well.''

''It's all part of being an attorney. Knowing what makes people tick.''

''I find that important in my work as a counselor, too.''

''Yes, I can see that you're an astute judge of character. And you have the warm, caring heart of a counselor.''

''Thank you.'' Bree absently twisted her paper napkin into a ragged rope. She wanted to know more about Eric and his family, but would he think she was prying? ''I cared deeply for your sister and wondered so often what kind of home she came from.''

Eric grimaced. ''I'll tell you this much. The defining moment in understanding my mother came when I was twenty. I was rummaging through some old papers in the attic one day and found her marriage certificate.''

''I don't understand. How did that help?''

Eric was silent for a moment, conflicting emotions playing out on his face. When he spoke again, his voice took on a subdued, lachrymose strain. ''I discovered my parents got married less than six months before I was born. It hit me like a ton of bricks. My mother, the consummate, unimpeachable perfectionist, had to get married. Incredible irony, right? I never breathed a word about it to anyone. Not even to Marnie. But that's why my mother hovered over Marnie so much, always scolding and domineering, warning her till she was blue in the face about the dangers of male companionship.''

Bree emitted a low whistle. ''No wonder Marnie refused to let her mother know she was pregnant.''

"I'm afraid my mother's constant nagging and belittling turned out to be a self-fulfilling prophecy. Like mother, like daughter."

"It's too bad Marnie didn't know her mother had lived through the same experience. She wouldn't have felt so alone and unredeemable."

Eric nodded solemnly. "Yes, we all have a lot of regrets when it comes to my sister."

"But at least she came to know the Lord. She knew she was forgiven. She found the unconditional love she had longed for all her life."

"Yes, I'm thankful for that." Eric nodded toward the infant carrier. "And I didn't realize I'd feel this way, but I'm thankful for that little one. Marnie's still alive in her."

Tears welled in Brianna's eyes. "That's how I feel, too. When I look at Charity, I think of Marnie and how much she loved her little daughter. That's why it's so important that we find the perfect home for her."

Eric shrugged, tight-lipped for a moment. "There's no perfect home, Bree, but I have lined up some interviews with prospective parents."

Bree felt a flutter of surprise...and something else. What was it? Alarm? Disappointment? "You've already made appointments to interview couples? When?"

"Monday afternoon, if you're available."

"Yes, I can be. Where? Your office?"

"Right. At 2:00 p.m. I contacted the couples we discussed the other night. The ones we felt were most promising."

Bree struggled to gather her thoughts. What was wrong that this news distressed her? "It's just that...I mean, I know we looked at lots of adoption applications, and, yes, we commented on some of them, but I didn't realize you would act so quickly."

Eric sat forward, his handsome features registering perplexity and concern. "You do want to find Charity a good home, don't you?"

"Yes, of course, but..."

Charity stirred and made a soft mewling sound, as if she realized she was the subject of this portentous conversation. Bree reached into the infant carrier, lifted the squirming infant, and gently positioned Charity on her shoulder and tucked the pink flannel blanket around her. "There, there, sweetheart, everything's okay."

Charity made a few whimpering sounds, then relaxed and grew quiet, as Bree nuzzled her silky head and crooned a muffled lullaby.

"You sure have a way with her," noted Eric with undisguised admiration. "You've gone beyond the call of duty, taking care of my sister's baby as if she were your own."

"It's not a duty," said Bree. "I love taking care of her."

"I can see that. But you can't keep her indefinitely. You told me so yourself. You have a demanding career, a busy, productive life, with no room for an infant."

Bree kissed Charity's satiny hair. "I know, but I...I'm getting used to having her around."

Eric's expression softened. "She is a treasure, isn't she."

Before Brianna could reply, her attention was diverted by a rustling sound in the grass. She looked around and spotted a middle-aged couple in blue sweats jogging toward them. As they approached the picnic table, they slowed their pace. The man loped by, but the woman—a stout yet attractive matron with cropped, gray-streaked hair—stopped and gazed at the baby.

"Oh, Fred, look! Isn't this baby a little doll!"

Fred stopped a few yards away, panting heavily and looking mildly exasperated. "Come on, Frieda! Leave the kid alone!"

The woman waved him away. "Oh, Fred, I just want to look at her for a minute."

Rubbing a fine mist of perspiration from her neck, Frieda stole closer and hovered expectantly over Brianna. She reeked of strong perfume, a heavy floral scent.

"You don't mind, do you, dear? Just one little peek?"

Bree nudged the blanket away from Charity's sleeping face.

"Oh, she's the cutest little thing! It is a girl, isn't it? Pink blanket, but you never know these days."

"Yes, a girl," said Bree, silently praying the woman's shrill voice wouldn't startle the baby out of a sound sleep.

The woman steepled her pudgy fingers, as if in prayer, and lavished Brianna with a beatific smile. "What a lovely little family! Mommy, Daddy and darling baby girl! Isn't God good?"

"Oh, we're not—" Bree began, then let the words die on her lips. How could she explain to this stranger that they were the furthest thing from a family?

Frieda placed a hand self-assuredly on Brianna's shoulder, as if bestowing a blessing. "You listen to me, dear. Love your husband with all your heart. Don't let anything distract you. Give him all the love you've got. Someday the two of you will be married for over thirty years, like Fred and me. Keep your little family together always, just like this. You'll never be sorry.''

Suddenly Fred piped up, his gravelly voice ringing with a mixture of irony and impatience. ''And listen here, folks. Someday you'll be married for over thirty years like me and my nosy wife...if I don't strangle her first.''

''Oh, Fred, you old grouch! I'm not nosy. Just friendly.''

''And I'm the King of Siam. Come on. Leave the lovebirds alone. They don't need you fawning over them and their kid.''

Frieda drew back reluctantly, her gaze darting from Charity to Fred. Finally she looked at Bree and made an exaggerated sad face. ''I better go. Take care of that little angel. And take care of each other. You've got a sweet little family. It doesn't get any better than that.''

''Thank you,'' Bree replied, as the woman fell into step beside her husband. The two joined hands and broke into a slow trot, running side by side, the echo of their voices wafting back on the warm summer air.

''She thought we were married—a real family,'' said Bree, a pleasant warmth flooding her cheeks. ''I couldn't tell her—''

Eric shifted his torso. ''Sure. Why spoil it for her?''

''I never stopped to think. I mean, it's so ironic, isn't it. The three of us are heading in totally different directions, and yet we looked like a...like a family.''

''*Twilight Zone* time,'' Eric quipped lamely. He was drumming his fingers on the table in a steady, marching cadence, as if seized by a restless energy.

''I'm sorry. I didn't mean to make you feel uncomfortable. It just startled me to have a stranger think of us that way.''

"No problem. "It's just that the idea of marriage, a family, is so far removed from my reality. Let's just say it's the last thing on my priority list."

"Oh, same here," Bree assured him. "I've got too much going on to think about a family." She rocked Charity in her arms, as if to quiet her, although the infant was slumbering peacefully. After a moment she ventured, "Is it because of your parents?"

Eric arched one eyebrow. "Is *what* because of my parents?"

Bree groped for words. "Your feelings about marriage. Your desire to remain a bachelor. Did your parents disillusion you?"

"Who says I'm disillusioned?"

"Nobody. I just thought—" Heaven help her, she was feeling more foolish and humiliated by the minute.

"I just haven't given marriage much thought. It's not on my agenda, at least not for the next five years or so."

"I'm in no hurry to marry, either," Brianna agreed, oddly feeling the need to defend herself to this man who was practically a stranger to her. "I couldn't possibly squeeze in a family, especially now, knowing how much work a baby is."

Eric was still drumming his fingers on the table, the beat growing louder, more forceful. He looked grimly preoccupied, his thoughts traveling some outer perimeter of the universe.

"I suppose it could have something to do with my parents," he conceded. "For as long as I can remember, I've vowed never to do to my children what my mother did to Marnie and me. If that means not getting married at all, so be it."

"But you wouldn't be that kind of father," protested

Bree. "You would be loving and kind. I see that in you."

"Then, you know me better than I know myself, Miss Rowlands," he said with an edge of irony in his voice.

Why had he lapsed back into formalities, calling her "Miss Rowlands"? "I'm not trying to be argumentative," she assured him. "It's just that…it would be a shame to deny yourself a family because of the way you were raised."

Eric scrutinized her. "Are you trying to convince me to raise Charity myself? Is that what this conversation is about? If you are, let me remind you I'm a single man with nothing to offer a child."

Nothing except love, Bree wanted to say. Instead, she mumbled under her breath, "It's just a shame Charity will never know any of her real family."

"Her real family is the one that will adopt her." Eric stood abruptly and began packing the food in the basket.

Bree could see that she had upset him. You might know. She and her big mouth. Why hadn't she just left well enough alone?

Eric straightened his shoulders. "Time to go, Miss Rowlands. We have several couples to interview tomorrow. I'm convinced one of them will be the ideal family for Charity."

Chapter Nine

The next morning, Brianna and Eric spent several tense and exhausting hours at his law office interviewing prospective parents for Charity. Bree had assumed the interviews would be a piece of cake. How hard could it be? Simply talk to some nice folks and find the best family for Charity. Easy. *Not!*

By the time they had finished conversing with three couples, Bree was fit to be tied. Naturally, she had let Eric do most of the talking; he was the attorney, after all. But occasionally she had voiced a question or two, the kinds of questions perhaps only a woman would ask. When Charity is feeling sad and lonely, how will you let her know you love her? What will you tell her someday about her birth mother? How will you react when she makes choices that disappoint you?

Most of the couples gave suitable answers, but what surprised Bree most of all was her own internal response. The idea of strangers being there for Charity, comforting her, telling her about her birth mother, and impacting her future, left Bree feeling an enormous void in her chest and a sob in her throat that simply wouldn't dissolve.

She prayed as one couple left and another arrived, Please, Lord, just let me get through this ordeal without crying!

After everyone had left and she and Eric were alone in his office, Brianna sank down in a leather armchair and heaved a sigh of relief. "Thank goodness, that's over! I feel like I was just put through a wringer, and I wasn't even the one answering the questions."

Eric was sitting at his desk, leaning on his elbows, his fingers tented under his chin. He looked astonishingly debonair in a three-piece, gray pinstripe suit. "Yes, it's grueling. I feel the same way. I want to be sure we pick the right parents for Charity. Her whole life is at stake here."

Bree pressed her moist palms against her flushed cheeks. "That doesn't make me feel any better. What if we make a mistake? What if we give Charity to people who won't love her as much as we do?"

A peculiar expression crossed Eric's face, as if he hadn't realized until just now that he did actually love the child.

"You do care about her, too, don't you," said Bree. "I can see it in your face. It's just as hard for you to think about letting her go as it is for me."

Eric rocked back in his chair and folded his arms across his chest. "That's not the issue, Brianna. Our feelings don't count. We have to make a rational choice based on the evidence."

"Now you're sounding like a lawyer again."

"I *am* a lawyer."

"I didn't mean that as an insult or a criticism. It's

just…no matter what the evidence shows, how can we be sure we make the right decision?''

His eyes crinkled at the corners and took on that warm look she loved. ''Prayer helps. We trust God to bring us the right parents for Charity. And we trust Him to give us wisdom to recognize them when we meet them.''

''You make it sound so easy.'' Bree shifted in her chair, crossing her legs at the knee. She was wearing a fitted, dusty-rose coatdress with a spread collar, an antique cameo at her throat. What she wanted to say was, *When the time comes, how do I let Charity go? How do I fill the void in my life she'll leave when she's gone?*

''A penny for your thoughts,'' mused Eric. ''Or, inflation being what it is, I'll raise that to a dollar.''

The heat rose in Bree's cheeks. ''It's nothing. I was just thinking of Charity, and how much I want the best for her.''

''So do I,'' said Eric with a surprising little rumble of emotion in his voice. ''For Marnie's sake.''

Bree nodded. ''Yes, for Marnie.''

Eric tented his fingers again, as if his professional stance would ward off any danger of his emotions surfacing again. ''So what did you think, Brianna? Of the couples we interviewed? See any likely candidates?''

With effort, she forced her mind into its most rational, dispassionate mode. ''I thought all the couples were basically nice people.''

''Okay, so far so good.''

''But none of them had that…that spark, that magic, that charisma that told me they were the one.''

''Spark? Magic? Charisma? Bree, they're not auditioning for Broadway. This is parenthood we're talking about, not Ringling Brothers.''

"I know." She absently fingered her cameo. "I'm not asking for Cinderella and Prince Charming in an enchanted castle."

"I should hope not. Fantasy doesn't cut it in the real world of parenting."

"But there should be more. All right, I'm an impossible optimist, a dreamer like the rest of my family, like my dad. But Charity needs more than two people who are going to send her to the most prestigious schools, and make sure she has her own savings account by age two and a stock portfolio by age twelve."

"Okay, you're talking about that one couple, the Brysons. That's not what they said, exactly. A portfolio by the time she's sixteen, I think they said. Besides, there's nothing wrong with a couple making plans for their child's financial future."

"Of course not, as long as they love her. But they never mentioned love. Where love should be, they see dollar signs!"

Eric thrummed his fingers on his wide mahogany desk. "Maybe you're right about them. But what about the Wrights? Now, they seemed like a loving couple."

Bree nodded. "I liked them. And I felt sorry for them. They said they lost a baby last year. Crib death. Three months old. I can tell they're still hurting."

"So maybe Charity can fill the empty place in their hearts."

"I know that's how they see it, Eric, but is it fair for them to expect Charity to fill a vacuum left by another child? They even want to rename her Elizabeth, after the baby who died. But what if they're disappointed when they realize Charity isn't Elizabeth and never can be. Don't you see, Eric? You can't replace one child with another."

suffering from post-traumatic stress disorder and other physical and mental health problems. And there are the soldiers from the Gulf War exposed to Agent Orange. I make sure their rights are properly represented in the courts.''

Brianna tightened her hold on Eric's arm. ''I'm impressed. I had no idea you were such a charitable, altruistic man.''

''Don't pin any medals on me yet. In the courtroom I can be just as competitive and cutthroat as the next guy. I like to win, and I like a good fight. But I also like to make sure the underdog gets a fair shake.''

''Sounds good to me.''

They arrived at the Gray Wolf Bistro, a cozy restaurant with red café curtains, linen-draped tables with fresh flowers, and pale blue walls covered with bold Mondrian prints. The hostess showed them to a small table in the corner, where they ordered Caesar salads and poached salmon with dill sauce.

Bree spread her linen napkin over her lap. ''My goodness, Eric, when you suggested lunch, I pictured a burger and fries.''

''Yes, if I were eating alone. But you don't seem like a burger-and-fries sort of girl. Quesadillas, yes. Burgers, no.''

She laughed lightly. ''Oh, but I am. I'm just a simple girl. When I'm home I love going barefoot and wearing my old grubbies and my hair in long braids.''

He grinned, a mischievous gleam in his eyes. ''I would love to see you looking like that sometime.''

''Not on your life!''

''Well, maybe someday I'll drop in and surprise ou.''

''Right again, Brianna. I suppose being a counselor gives you an edge when it comes to intuition and discernment.''

''Are you saying that sincerely, or is there a hint of sarcasm in your voice?''

''No, I mean it. You've got the market cornered on perspicacity.''

She laughed. ''Are you kidding? I can't even say it! Per...what?''

''It means wisdom. Insight. What I'm trying to say is, I like your sensitivity. You see life with all the subtle shades of gray, while I try to pigeonhole everything into black or white. The letter-of-the-law type of thing.''

''So are you saying you think the Wrights should adopt Charity?''

''Didn't say that. Don't think it, either. But I liked them better than the Crowders. They couldn't agree on anything.''

Bree stifled a chuckle. ''He wants a boy, she wants a girl.''

''She wants a baby, he wants an older child.''

''I have a feeling Charity would find herself pulled in opposite directions all her life. We can't inflict that on her.''

Eric picked up a pen and tapped it on his desk. ''Okay. So the Crowders are crossed off our list. We still have other couples to interview, if you want to come back another day.''

''Yes. I've got to see this through. I owe it to Marnie.''

''Okay, I'll let you know when.''

She clasped her handbag and stood up. ''Then, I guess I should let you get to work.''

He set down the pen and gave her a quizzical smile.

"Tell you what. Let me tie up a few loose ends here, and I'll take you to lunch."

"Oh, you don't have to do that."

"I want to. It'll give us a chance to chat some more about Charity. I'd like to spend some more time with her before…well, before we find her a new home. For my sister's sake. The little tyke is the closest thing I still have to Marnie. The truth is, she makes losing my sister a little less painful."

"I feel the same way. Charity is so full of life. When I rock her and sing to her, it's as if Marnie is still here."

"She is, Brianna. I feel it, too." Eric cleared his throat uneasily, as if struggling to keep his emotions in check, and reached for his telephone. "Let me make a few quick calls, and we'll be on our way." His businesslike voice again.

Brianna walked over to the window and looked out, while Eric made his calls. But she couldn't help overhearing his side of the conversation. She admired his capable, take-charge tone as he doled out advice and resolved one problem after another.

Finally he hung up the receiver and swiveled his chair toward her. "I'm sorry to keep you waiting. Ready to go?"

"Yes, and please don't apologize. It's interesting, seeing you work. You have a marvelous way about you. I'm sure you could accomplish anything you set your mind to."

He chuckled, and she noticed a slight flush in his cheeks. "Keep talking like that, Miss Rowlands, and you'll make my day."

She smiled. "You're supposed to call me Brianna. Or Bree."

"You're right, absolutely right. Bree is short and

sweet, but I think I'll go with Brianna. It ha[s] musical sound."

Now it was her turn to blush. "Keep it up, M[r.] gate, and you'll make my day, too."

"We've done away with the formalities, remem[ber.] He got up and came around his desk. Gently he tou[ched] her elbow. "There's a wonderful bistro down the st[reet.] They have mouth-watering steak sandwiches, delici[ous] salmon and cheesecake that melts in your mouth."

She slipped her arm in his. "You've said the mag[ic] words."

They left Eric's office and stepped out into the balmy air and sunshine. "It's close. We could walk if you like."

"Sounds good to me." As they crossed the parking lot to the sidewalk, she said, "Eric, when you were on the phone, I couldn't help listening."

"Ah, an eavesdropper! What did you hear that piqued your interest?"

"Nothing, really. It's just that you were talking with a Vietnam vet one minute and Family Court the next. You obviously have quite a varied clientele."

"I like it that way. I suppose most people see me as a high-powered, high-energy attorney, a corporate liti[gator] with a big, impersonal firm. But that's not whe[re] my heart is. I love doing pro bono work whenever I c[an] fit it in."

"What all do you do?"

"Volunteer at the local Legal Aid Clinic, arra[nge] adoptions for pregnant teens, just like I'm doi[ng] Marnie's baby. And in my spare time—what the[re] it—I help out at the local VFW post."

"VFW?"

"Veterans of Foreign Wars. I represent Vi[etnam]

"You're welcome anytime, but please call first. Let me maintain a shred of dignity."

"To tell you the truth, I'm no etiquette king myself. I like to watch football in my pajamas with a heaping bowl of microwave popcorn beside me."

"Oh, I love popcorn! I could make a meal of it."

"Sometimes I do."

Their order came then, so for a while they concentrated on their food. When they were nearly finished, Eric said, "If you don't mind, Brianna, I'd like to stop by again and see Charity."

"Of course. I know she'd love to see you."

"I'm getting quite fond of the little tot. I know she won't remember me after she's adopted, but maybe somewhere deep in her mind she'll carry a mental picture of me."

"I know what you mean. I keep hoping she'll remember how much she was loved right from the beginning."

"Somehow, I have a feeling she will."

Bree poked at her salmon. "And I pray that she'll have parents who tell her about Jesus and how much He loves her."

A shadow crossed Eric's face. "How can we be sure of that? We'll never really know, will we."

"We can make sure she's adopted by a Christian family."

"Yes, that goes without saying. The couples we've interviewed all have Christian backgrounds to one degree or another. But whether they'll communicate to Charity that Christ wants to have a personal relationship with her, I don't know."

"I guess we'll just have to leave it in God's hands."

"Meanwhile, I'm looking forward to spending some quality time with my little niece."

"That'll be great. When would you like to come over?"

"How about the weekend? Is Saturday good for you?"

Brianna felt a sweet ripple of anticipation. "Saturday? Sure. Perfect."

The following Saturday Eric showed up shortly after breakfast and made a day of it. He and Bree took Charity to the park again and had a picnic lunch under the elms. And as the weeks of September slipped by, Saturday became a regular thing, and then Sundays, and Wednesdays. Eric and Brianna slowly settled into a pleasant limbo, behaving as if they were a family, as if Charity were theirs. Finding parents to adopt her somehow lost its urgency. And yet the unsettling truth lurked in the shadows of every hour they spent together. Brianna couldn't deny it. She and Eric were playing family, but they weren't Charity's parents and never could be. They were deluding themselves, and yet neither desired to end the charade.

What Brianna could never divulge to Eric was how deeply she cherished their times together, not just for Charity's sake, but for her own. The infatuation that had budded months ago when she gazed at Eric's photograph blossomed into profound affection for a man of integrity and compassion, a man who loved the Lord as much as she did. In fact, if she dared admit it to herself, she was in love with Eric Wingate—hopelessly, utterly in love. But around Eric she was careful never to hint of her feelings—for hadn't he made it clear from the beginning that he had no desire for a family of his own?

As each day passed, Bree felt more conflicted. She

knew that she and Eric ought to decide on a family for Charity. They had certainly interviewed enough couples, and there were many who would provide a good upbringing. She owed it to Charity to get her into a permanent home as soon as possible, before she became too attached to Eric and her. So why was she procrastinating?

Somewhere in her heart she knew the answer, but it was too painful to acknowledge. She wanted Eric and Charity for herself. She loved them both and couldn't bring herself to let them go. And once Charity was placed in a permanent home, Eric would be gone, as well, for there would be no reason for him to visit, no excuse for their long walks in the park, their picnics, their wonderful outings every week. Just like that, in a heartbeat, she would lose two people she loved.

But by early October Bree had indulged her own wishes long enough. It was time to put Charity first. Do what was best for the child, no matter how devastating the consequences might be for Brianna. But could she summon the courage to put in motion the process that would take Charity away from her forever?

Chapter Ten

On the third Saturday of October—a crisp, sun-washed autumn day—Eric invited Brianna and Charity to accompany him to Julian, an historical gold-mining town in the mountains northeast of La Jolla. They left after breakfast in his luxury sedan, drove through the lush countryside of North San Diego County, and arrived in the quaint tourist town within the hour.

Eric parked beside the cider mill on vintage Main Street, its rustic shops and cottages, with their antiquated clapboard storefronts reminiscent of a scene from an old John Wayne movie. The moment Bree stepped from the car she breathed in the tangy sweet fragrance of apples and cider. "Oh, I love this place already!" she crooned.

Eric reached into the back seat and lifted Charity out of her infant seat. She was still slumbering contentedly, as he fastened her into the corduroy carrier on his chest. Startled, her blue eyes opened wide for a moment, then she snuggled back against him. "Looks like she's happy," he mused.

Bree gently stroked the baby's plump red cheek. "Now if she just stays that way while we shop..."

"Well, let's not waste any time. Where shall we start?"

Bree smoothed her green velveteen shirt over her matching stretch jeans. The air was just cool enough that she was glad she had worn long sleeves. Eric, looking like a seasoned ranch hand in his denim jacket and jeans, blended handsomely with the old western motif. "Everything looks so inviting," said Bree, "but I can't resist the yummy smells coming from the cider mill."

"I'm game, Bree. Let's go in."

As they stepped inside the little shop, the tempting aromas of caramel apples, fruit marmalade and apple butter surrounded them. "Oh, Eric, I want a taste of everything!"

He chuckled. "Ah, indigestion, here we come!" He bought two caramel apples, a bag of cashews and two cups of cider. "You know, Bree, if we do this at every shop, we'll need a moving van to cart us home."

Gingerly she sank her teeth into the warm caramel and crisp apple. Between bites, she mumbled, "I promise not to go hog-wild like this in every shop."

He squeezed her arm playfully. "That's reassuring."

Over the next few hours they explored nearly every weathered, picturesque store on the block: the candle shop, redolent with incense, where glimmering candles were created right in the store; the chocolate shop—a sugar oasis that could only be described as a chocolate lover's dream, and the candy store—brimming with fudge, saltwater taffy, licorice and maple; and the clown shop, filled with music boxes, mobiles, paintings and figurines. For lunch they stopped at the diner and drug store, a homespun 1886 historical brick building with a

1928 soda fountain surrounded by a plethora of old-time memorabilia.

They sat at a little oilcloth-covered table by the plate-glass window and devoured cheeseburgers and shakes. Charity woke halfway through their meal and began to squall, so Eric removed her from the carrier and handed her to Bree. "Looks like she needs a mother's touch."

"She's probably hungry and wet. I'll have the waitress warm her bottle."

"And I'll go get her diaper bag and stroller out of the trunk."

Within minutes Eric was back with the baby paraphernalia. While he polished off his burger, Brianna took Charity to the rest room and changed her in the cramped, airless space. But her efforts were rewarded when she returned to the table with a smiling, cooing baby.

"Well, she looks happy," said Eric, his smile matching Charity's.

Bree reached for the warmed baby bottle. "She'll be even happier when she's fed. I'm giving her a soybean formula now. It seems to agree with her better. She's not so colicky."

Charity curled herself in the curve of Brianna's arm—a plump, apple-cheeked pixie in a ruffled gown—and took the bottle eagerly, making loud, satisfied sucking noises.

Eric chuckled, a pleased sound high in his throat. "Did you see how she smiled when she saw that bottle coming at her? That wasn't gas. That was an honest-to-goodness, ear-to-ear grin."

Bree matched his bemused laughter. "You'll get no argument from me. This baby girl is one smart cookie.

Of course, she can smile, even if it's only a toothless grin.''

''Most beautiful toothless grin I ever saw.'' To Bree's amazement and delight, Eric sat forward, clucked Charity under the chin and began spouting baby talk.

Was it possible? Eric Wingate, the suave corporate attorney, crooning in an unsettling falsetto, ''How's my little sugarplum sweetums baby-doll girl?''

Bree and Eric were both tittering unabashedly over Charity's antics, when a woman at the next table leaned over and cooed in a honey-sweet voice, ''You two have the cutest little baby! And she looks just like her daddy!''

Both Brianna and Eric were too startled to reply with anything other than a stricken ''thank you.'' Bree glanced around self-consciously and realized that half of the restaurant's patrons were looking their way, many flashing blissful smiles in Charity's direction. ''Looks like we're a hit,'' Bree whispered. ''Or should I say, Charity's a hit.''

Eric's ears reddened. ''I'm not used to this daddy routine. Maybe it's time to make our escape.''

''Let me burp her first.'' Bree held Charity up on her shoulder and thumped her back, her fingers feeling instinctively for the spot that would release a belch. How could she tell Eric that she had no desire to leave this place, that she enjoyed the image they portrayed of a happy family? *Father, mother, baby girl. Let me enjoy the fantasy a little longer,* she begged silently.

But Eric was already pulling out his wallet to pay the bill. Reluctantly, Bree laid Charity in the stroller and gathered her purse and diaper bag.

When they stepped outside, she caught the heavy

smell of rain in the air. The late-afternoon sun had faded
to a pale orange globe straining its faded rays through
low scudding clouds.

"Should we head home?" she asked Eric.

"No way. We came for the day, and it's not over
yet." He glanced over at Bree as they headed for the
pioneer museum on the corner of Washington and
Fourth. "Do you think it's true?"

"What's true?"

"That Charity looks like me."

A tickle of merriment traveled along Bree's spine.
"Of course she looks like you. You're her uncle."

"Yes, but that doesn't necessarily mean—"

"Take my word for it. She's the spitting image of
you."

He eyed her skeptically. "You're baiting me, right?"

"No, I'm not. She definitely favors you. Why
wouldn't she? Your sister was her mother. If we're talking bloodlines, you can't get much closer than that."

Eric's lips settled into a tight, gratified smile. He was
obviously pleased as punch, but he didn't say another
word until they had reached the museum. Then, without
looking at Bree, he murmured under his breath, "Sometimes I feel like her daddy."

Bree's pulse quickened. "What did you say?"

Eric shook his head and reached for the stroller.
"Nothing important. We'd better head inside if we want
to catch the sights. The museum will be closing soon."

But as he pushed the stroller through the door, Bree
followed with a pang of disappointment. Her hopes had
soared for an instant when Eric had said, *Sometimes I
feel like her daddy.* She had wanted to cry, *Yes, and I
feel like her mother! Doesn't that mean the three of us
belong together?*

But, of course, it meant no such thing. She and Eric and Charity looked like a family and acted like a family and sometimes even talked like a family. But it was all a mirage, a fantasy, a painful illusion. Eric was spending time with Bree just to be near Charity. And one of these days she would wake from this marvelous dream and find herself painfully alone.

Bree heard little of the tour guide's stories about Julian's short-lived gold rush and the pioneers who had farmed the land and planted countless orchards of apple trees. Charity had awakened and was fussy, and Bree's mind was still echoing Eric's words, *Sometimes I feel like her daddy.*

Oh please, Lord, she prayed silently. *Please let it be! As impossible as it sounds, please let Eric and me raise Charity!*

After the museum, they took a ride around town in a horse-drawn carriage. The rhythmic sway of the buggy and the clippity-clop of the horses' hooves lulled Charity back to sleep. The sun had become an orange, succulent melon hugging the horizon. A breeze was stirring and the cloud layer had dropped.

Bree held out her palm. "It feels like rain."

"No, not tonight. It's a perfect evening. And going to get better."

"Better? How could it get any better?"

"We have one more event on our agenda. I think you'll like it."

"Really? Tell me."

"We're going to a popular dinner theater near Julian. A comedy is playing. Can't recall the name, but it's a local acting troupe. Talented, professional. There's a barbecue dinner at six-thirty…chicken, baby back pork ribs, salad bar, the works. Curtain's at eight. What do you say?''

''Sounds terrific. But what about Charity? What if she fusses?''

''We'll sit in the back and keep her in her stroller. I bet she'll sleep through the whole thing.''

''If you're willing to chance it, so am I. Sounds like fun. And I have been rather housebound since Charity came to stay, so a night at the theater would be wonderful.''

''Then, let's go. We should have just enough time to give Charity her bottle and get to the theater for the dinner hour.''

To Brianna's delight, the evening went just like clockwork. Charity took her bottle eagerly and slept through the scrumptious barbecue dinner and the zany stage show. This gave Bree and Eric a pleasant and uninterrupted evening together in the rustic lodge with its massive stone fireplace and homespun log furniture.

But the moment they stepped outside after the show, Bree knew they were in trouble. The pleasant, temperate weather had given way to pelting rain and a rolling fog bank. Holding Charity's blanket over their heads, they ran to the car, deposited her into her car seat and clambered into their seats, slamming the car doors against the downpour. As Eric turned the ignition, Bree shook the water from her dampened tresses.

''I told you it looked like rain,'' she murmured with a little shiver. Her velveteen outfit was soaking wet and water squeaked in her casual pumps.

''When you're right, you're right,'' he conceded as he pulled out onto the flooded highway. His headlights carved only a meager hole in the fog, and the windshield wipers swished vainly against the relentless torrent.

"I can't see a thing," Bree complained, sitting forward, her neck taut, her eyes squinting into the thick, swirling mists. "Eric, how can we drive home through this?"

He was craning his neck forward, too, his jaw tight with concentration. "We can't. We'd better find a place to stay."

"What about the lodge we just came from?"

"The sign said they were filled for the night. No Vacancy."

"Then, where, Eric? In this pea soup we can hardly see the front of the car."

"I'm taking Highway 78 back into downtown Julian. There has to be a place there."

As they drove, rain battered the sedan's roof and the damp wind seeped into its joints and seams and crevices. Bree shivered, wishing she had brought a jacket or a change of clothes. How could they spend the night somewhere, when they had no toiletries, no provisions, no dry clothing? Had she even brought enough formula for Charity?

The fog was moving in with alarming swiftness, a swirling, ghostly white vapor broken only by the spiking rain, like something alive slithering over the darkened earth. Slowing the sedan to five miles an hour, Eric inched along through the gloom. Oncoming headlights cut shimmering circles of light in the shadowy miasma. In the distance sirens sounded, alerting the silent, cloistered world that someone was in trouble.

"We've got to stop soon," warned Bree. "We can't even see the road ahead."

"I know, but all I see are No Vacancy signs."

"Maybe we should stop the car somewhere and wait until the rain stops and the fog clears."

"That could be all night. I'm not letting you and Charity spend the night in a cold, damp car. It's not safe."

Bree tried to keep the anxiety out of her voice. "Then, what are we going to do?"

"Look, there, ahead. The Julian Lodge. It says, Vacancy."

Through the drizzle and shadows Bree spotted the sprawling, two-story bed-and-breakfast on a sloping hill. "A shelter in the time of storm. Thank God!"

Eric pulled into the nearly filled parking lot and stopped near the office. "Now, let's just hope they're open."

Bree gazed around at the bevy of automobiles. "It looks like everyone else has the same idea. No one wants to be out in this weather."

Eric opened his door. "You stay here and keep the door locked. I'll see about getting us a couple of rooms." He disappeared into the office and was gone for nearly ten minutes. When he returned he was carrying a key and a receipt.

Bree's heart leapt. "You did it!"

Eric leaned inside the vehicle, his thick hair dripping with rain, his forehead creased. "Not quite what we wanted. They had only one room left."

"You took it, didn't you?"

"Of course. But it may be a little crowded with the three of us."

"I'm not worrying about propriety or comfort tonight. I just want to get off the road and inside where it's safe."

"Then, let's go. Here's the key. First floor, room 12. Get the lights and heat on, and I'll get Charity."

Within minutes they were settled inside the cozy room with its pink wallpaper, bell-jar lamps, four-poster double bed and antique furniture. As the heater spewed warmth into the room, Bree laid a slumbering Charity on the ruffled comforter and changed her, then put a fresh receiving blanket in the infant seat and gently tucked her in. She placed the carrier on the floor beside the bed.

"I think she'll sleep through the night. She's had such a big day."

Eric slipped off his damp denim jacket. "Haven't we all."

"You're soaked." Bree shivered and placed her cold hands over the toasty heater.

"You, too. Soaked to the skin. Who would have thought we'd need a change of clothes?"

"We could put our things on the heater. They shouldn't take long to dry."

Eric's right brow arched sharply. "And in the meantime, we wear...what? Our birthday suits?"

Bree felt a blush creep up her cheeks. "There must be extra blankets. We can wrap ourselves in them until our clothes are ready."

Eric sighed and began unbuttoning his shirt. "I never intended to put you in such a compromising situation. I was sure we could get two rooms."

"It's okay. We'll survive. But I should call my dad."

Eric looked around. "Afraid not. No phones."

"There's more than one way to phone home." Bree retrieved her cell phone from her purse and punched in the number, then shook her head. "Battery's gone. You might know."

He grimaced, his eyes conveying sympathy. "Makes you feel cut off from the rest of the world, doesn't it?"

She sat down on the bed and kicked off her dripping shoes. "It does. Like we're caught in a time warp."

Eric spread his wet shirt over one section of the heater. He then sat down in the overstuffed armchair beside the bed and removed his leather boots, while Bree fetched two spare blankets from the small closet. She handed him one.

"These should do the job."

He nodded toward the bathroom. "You first."

"Thanks. I won't be long." She grabbed her purse, glad she carried a spare toothbrush in her cosmetics bag. She washed, flossed her teeth and brushed her long tawny hair into a lustrous cascade of slightly damp curls. She removed her velveteen outfit and wrapped the flannel blanket around herself, then made her grand entrance.

"I feel like a mummy. All wrapped up and no place to go."

Eric gave her a sweeping glance. He couldn't seem to hold back an approving smile. "You look like a little girl. Cute as a bug in a rug."

"Thanks, I think." She inched her way over to the bed and sat down on the fluffy comforter. "Your turn."

Eric picked up the remote control and snapped on the TV to a country-western station. "Thought you might want some entertainment." A male quartet was singing something about facing the barren waste without a trace of water.

"Now, that's timely," she quipped. "All we have is water, water, everywhere."

"Let's hope it lets up by morning." Eric took his turn in the bathroom, and emerged wrapped in his blanket, his dark hair toweled and the shadow of a beard on his chiseled jaw.

Bree smiled. "You look like a Native American chief."

He tightened the blanket around his trim midriff, grinning. "I'm still trying to figure out how we ended up like this...bundled in blankets in a cozy little room in a blinding downpour. Didn't someone make a movie like this?"

"I think it's an old Clark Gable movie. Saw it when I was a teenager. Loved it."

He spread the rest of their clothes over the heater, then settled down in the overstuffed chair and stretched out his bare legs. "Guess we should get some shut-eye."

She studied him curiously, noticing the way the soft lamplight gave his classic features a golden glow. "Where are you going to sleep?" she asked quietly.

He shrugged. "Right here. Where else?"

"In that chair? It doesn't look very comfortable."

He gave her a long, appraising glance. "I'm trying to protect your honor, Brianna, in a rather tempting situation."

She felt that pleasant warmth in her face again. "I just meant...I'm sorry you weren't able to get another room."

"I don't mind. You get some sleep. I'll doze here in the chair, and by morning we should be on our way home."

Bree scooted down on the fleecy comforter, the blanket still twined around her, and fluffed the feather pillow under her head.

Eric clicked off the television and turned out the lamp. The small room was suddenly swallowed by silence and darkness. The air turned chill. In the shadowy stillness, the driving rain sounded jarringly loud. Fluid shapes writhed against the windowpanes like dancing phantoms, a quivering blend of wind, rain, lights and shadows.

After several minutes Brianna gazed over at Eric's strong, dark profile. "Are you asleep?" she whispered, rising up on one elbow.

He moved slightly, his arms crossed over his chest. "No, not yet. This chair isn't exactly conducive to slumber."

She hesitated a moment, then ventured, "You can lie here on the bed if you want. I trust you."

The air was charged with an uneasy silence, broken finally by Eric's gravelly voice. "Thanks, but no thanks. You may trust me, but it's going to be a long night, and I'm not sure I trust myself."

Startled, speechless, Bree rolled over and stared at the wall, disappointment pressing inside her chest. Was Eric so afraid of making even a fleeting connection with a woman that he would keep his distance at any cost? Did he think she had designs on him? That she was trying to entice him, seduce him? Surely he must know she had more pride than that.

But maybe he was right. She did yearn for his closeness. How she wished he would slip over and hold her in his arms through the long, dark night. Maybe he kept himself at a distance because he sensed subconsciously how much she cared for him. He had made it clear that he wanted no commitment. Why did she get her hopes up just because he was willing to spend time with her for Charity's sake?

And yet, he had said he wasn't sure he could trust himself. Did that mean he was attracted to her? Was he feeling the same warmth she felt…a yearning to be held and kissed and cherished?

"Brianna?" Eric's voice ended the silence.

Her heartbeat quickened. "Yes, Eric?"

"You asleep?"

"No. You?"

"Nope. Not sleepy."

"Me, neither."

"I'm just sitting here thinking…"

"About what?"

"Remembering…"

"Something good?"

"Remembering when Marnie and I were kids. I built a tree house. We slept in it one night when she was five and I was fifteen. It had no roof, so we could lie there and look up at the stars. At first she was scared to be outside in the dark, but whenever we heard a sound, I promised I'd protect her. Then I started pointing out all the stars, and she was fascinated. I felt like Superman. I could do anything. Protect my kid sister. Teach her about the stars. Man, what power I thought I had."

"You meant the world to her, Eric. She loved you so much."

"Yeah, I know. But now she's gone. I can't be that protective big brother anymore."

"There's still Charity."

"Yeah, Marnie's little girl. And what are we planning to do? Pawn her off on strangers."

In the darkness, Bree couldn't see Eric's face, but she heard the pain and turmoil in his voice. "It's not like that, Eric. We're doing our best to find Charity a good home."

"She should be with me," he said solemnly.

No, she should be with me! Brianna wanted to retort.

After a long, heart-pounding silence she ventured, "Are you thinking of keeping her?"

"How could I?" Eric returned. "I'm in no position to raise a child. She would end up with my parents, and I could never do that to Marnie's baby."

"I would keep her if I could," said Bree, "but I've already taken an extended leave from my counseling job."

"Who knows? Maybe we could work out joint custody." Eric sounded as if he might be making a joke— or was he testing the waters for her opinion?

"Joint custody? The two of us?"

"Why not? It's possible."

"But Charity needs a real home. A mother and father. We both agreed on that."

"You're right. It was a stupid idea. Forget I said it."

I don't want to forget, Bree wanted to shout. *Why can't you see what's staring you stark in the face? We belong together, the three of us! Eric, if only you loved me the way I love you!*

Eric broke into her reverie with a soft, chuckling sound. "It must be the stormy night, or the three of us being here in this strange place, but my mind is running a mile a minute. I can't stop dredging up all these memories from the past. Things I haven't thought about in years."

"I'm listening, Eric, if you feel like confiding."

"You don't want to hear all this stuff."

"Yes, I do. Every word."

"Okay, but only if you confide some of your youthful secrets, too. Is it a deal?"

"Deal."

For the next two hours, as the storm pounded its own sodden symphony, they swapped stories in the darkness—tales of fanciful adventures and dauntless dreams and youthful escapades. They talked about their hopes and prayers and fears and ambitions. Bree found herself sharing minutia about herself that she'd never shared with another living soul. And Eric spoke candidly of his troubled childhood, his formidable journey to faith in Christ, his ongoing emotional turmoil over Marnie's death, and his unresolved anger at his parents.

Finally, as the rain abated and the earth grew hushed, their conversation dwindled to mere monosyllables. By the first faint ribbons of dawn, Bree, swaddled in her blanket, and Eric, slumped in his overstuffed chair, had drifted into a deep, dreamless sleep.

Chapter Eleven

Andrew was worried. It was two in the morning, and still no sign of his daughter. She had taken Charity and gone out with Eric Wingate for the day. Mentioned driving to some tourist town in the country; he couldn't recall the name now. Why hadn't he written it down? She had promised to be home early; all right, not early exactly, but by a decent hour. He took that to mean nine or ten, especially since they were traveling with a baby. Brianna wouldn't want to keep Charity out late.

So why wasn't she home?

Why hadn't she called?

He had tried her cell phone, but it wasn't working.

Where was she on a miserable, stormy night like this?

Just before midnight, Andrew had phoned the Wingates on the unlikely chance they knew Eric's whereabouts. That was a faux pas. They let it be known that they didn't keep tabs on their son, that he rarely confided his activities to them, and that they didn't appreciate being awakened at midnight.

No wonder Marnie Wingate had run away from home.

Now, after calling the police and several local hospitals, Andrew was pacing the floor of his living room, trying not to worry.

Fat chance of that!

Earlier tonight, in a Bible study in this very room with a handful of his most faithful parishioners, hadn't he talked about trusting God in the most ordinary events of one's life? Oh, preach it, brother! Yes, indeed, he'd been at his most eloquent. Even Juliana had said so. "Inspiring!" That's what she'd called him. *Andrew, you are the most inspiring man I've ever met!*

And he'd lapped up every word.

Only one problem. He didn't live what he preached. Sure, it was easy to talk about trusting God. He could get downright grandiloquent on the subject. And he meant every word. God was absolutely trustworthy in every facet of life. He knew it. Believed it. No question.

And yet, since Mandy's death, and now after Marnie's, Andrew was holding on like a drowning man to everything he held dear, as if God might snatch away more than He had already taken, as if the Almighty took pleasure in inflicting pain on His children.

No, it didn't work that way. God was a God of love and joy and peace. He wanted the best for His children. He did nothing capriciously. He was the Good Shepherd who went an extra mile for His flock, who rescued them from the enemy and wept with them when they were hurting. His comfort was available to Andrew even now, if he was willing to accept it.

Then why was he being so pigheaded, relying on his own strength instead of God's?

"When I am weak, then am I strong."

But only when my weakness propels me into the arms of God can God's strength be perfected in my frailties.

Lord, I'm sorry, he acknowledged silently as he gazed out the bay window at the slanting rain. *I trust You for the big things, like my eternal salvation, but I sure have trouble with the little things, like my daughter's safety on a stormy night. Please let Brianna be all right. Haven't we had enough losses around here? I'm not trying to tell You how to do Your job, but I could sure use some peace of mind right now.*

"Andrew, is there any news?"

He whirled around, startled. Juliana, in a shapely red pantsuit, was standing by the sofa, where she had been dozing for the past hour. Her thick, ebony hair was tousled. She had stayed after the Bible study to keep him company until Brianna arrived home. Now it was so late, she would have to spend the night.

"No word yet," he said, going to her.

She went easily into his arms. He caught the fragrance of summer roses.

"I am so sorry, Andrew. You must be beside yourself with worry. Where could she be?"

"I don't know. I was so sure she would have called by now."

They sat down on the sofa, his arm circling her shoulders. It felt good, reassuring to have her in his arms, the solid reality of her against him, like a promise that good things could still happen. For weeks, now, they had prayed about their future together; they had danced around the reality of their love for each other. And yet they were still at square one—nothing decided, nothing official. He wanted to marry her, and yet he hadn't said the words.

The closest he had come was that day at La Jolla

Cove. They had confessed their love for each other and had spoken of the possibility of Juliana becoming a minister's wife…his wife. They had agreed to pray about it. And since then, they had prayed numerous times. *Lord, if You want us together, loving each other and serving You as a team, give us Your peace. Don't let us run ahead of You just to indulge our own desires.*

Andrew didn't know why he was dragging his feet about this marriage thing. Was he still waiting for God to direct him? To give him a special sign? Were his own fears sabotaging him? Was he holding back, afraid that if he allowed himself to love someone again, God might take her away, too? He couldn't bear another loss, especially a wife he loved with all his heart. But surely God wouldn't ask him to endure that kind of bereavement a second time. Or would He?

He was back to that. Trust. How much did he trust God?

Obviously not enough. Some man of God *he* was. No one in his congregation would guess how timid he was with his trust. His timidity shamed him, robbed him of his joy. He yearned to be more joyful and exuberant, the way he imagined Christ of Galilee to have been. Jesus, generous and effusive with His love, demonstrative with His emotions, giving freely of Himself, living life with a passion that prompted like emotion in others. He lived His passion even unto death, passion for His Father-God, compassion for the human race.

Jesus loved with perfect love…and perfect love casts out fear. God, why can't I love that way? Holding nothing back?

"Andrew, are you okay? You look so solemn, so distracted."

He rubbed Juliana's shoulder, his preoccupation dissolving. "No, I'm fine. Just thinking. And praying. Wondering where on earth Brianna could be."

"I am sure she's fine. Maybe they stopped somewhere for the night rather than risking the drive home."

"Then, why hasn't she called?"

"Maybe she assumes you went to bed and won't miss her until morning."

He smiled grimly. "Always an answer for everything, my darling Jewel. What would I do without you?"

Smiling back at him, she blew a little kiss into the air. "You will never find out, because I am here to stay."

"Are you?" He studied her intently. "That's my prayer, you know. God willing…"

She turned to face him, so close he could feel the honeyed warmth of her breath. "You make it too complicated, Andrew, when it is so simple. Why do you make it so difficult?"

"What? You mean us? Our relationship?"

"Yes. We love each other. We belong together. What can be more simple than that?"

He drew back slightly, wary, an alarm going off in his head. He wasn't ready to deal with this tonight, not now, not when his daughter was missing, maybe hurt, maybe dead. How could Juliana ask him to confront the question of their relationship at a time like this?

"This isn't the time, Juliana. I can't…"

"Oh, but you can, dear Andrew." In one smooth, fluid gesture, she clasped his face in her warm palms and brought her lips to his, moving her mouth over his with such a softness that for a moment he forgot his anxieties over his daughter.

His instincts took over for the next few moments as

he gathered Juliana into his arms and kissed her. Why was it that his anxieties set him on edge in other ways, made him vulnerable to his passions?

Scripture said it was better to marry than to burn with passion. But he didn't want his physical needs to push him into matrimony. No, it had to be God's will. God's timing. His spiritual motives had to be as strong as his physical yearnings. But how could he know the mind of God, when his beguiling Juliana sent his thoughts reeling and his heart pounding?

With her in his arms, he felt like a teenage boy again—awkward, overeager, out of control. And, oh, that was trouble with a capital *T!*

He released her and stood up unsteadily, with a little exclamation of dismay. "Oh, Juliana, what you do to me!"

Her laughter was musical. "Then, I have not lost my touch."

"No, you certainly haven't." It didn't help that they were here alone in his house in the middle of the night and that he was feeling in need of comfort and consolation.

"I'd better try the police again. Maybe they know something."

Juliana rose from the sofa and drifted over to him, her body moving with a natural grace. "You must not worry, Andrew. She will come home. God will take care of her."

He nodded and phoned the police, anyway.

"Nothing," he said minutes later as he hung up the receiver. Juliana was right again. Maybe it *was* time for him to trust her. And himself. And God. Time to plunge in, take the leap.

Pop the question.

He pulled Juliana back into his arms and searched her earthy brown eyes. "Do you believe God wants us together?" he asked, the words coming out more abrupt than he had intended.

"Yes, Andrew, I certainly do," she replied without the blink of an eye.

"Then, we should get married."

"Yes, I think we should."

"Then, it's settled."

"All right. If you say so."

"I do."

"Then, I do, too."

"Fine."

A tickle started somewhere in his stomach and spread throughout his frame, so that he had no choice but to vent it in explosive laughter. It was contagious, and soon Juliana was laughing, too. They laughed until they cried and had to stop and dry their eyes. They sat down on the sofa and hugged each other, and she rested her head on his shoulder while he smoothed back her silky, tangled hair.

They held each other for a long while, remnants of laughter still on their lips, still glazing their eyes. They kissed and laughed some more, and it was as if some great weight had been lifted from Andrew's shoulders, from his mind, from his heart. As if he had rolled some enormous burden from his back onto God's, and now he could rest and trust and enjoy all that the Lord had given him.

It was 3:00 a.m., and Brianna still wasn't home. But Andrew knew she was in good hands, as was he, and Juliana and all those he loved. His sense of relief was palpable. He hadn't felt so free and joyous since…since Mandy.

Yes, everything was in God's hands. And his own hands were finally open, unclenched, at ease.

Trusting.

pinable. Maybe it won't rain and spoil the Thanksgiving.

Frannie

Chapter Twelve

It started out to be the grandest Thanksgiving celebration Brianna had seen since her mother was alive. The
entire family was there—more than family—gathered
around the Rowlands' festive, turkey-laden table. Her
father and younger sister Frannie; Juliana and her
daughter Belina; and Bree's older sister Cassandra and
her husband, Antonio Pagliarulo, who was Juliana's
son. And, to Brianna's delight, Eric Wingate was there.
Like Bree, he didn't want to miss little Charity's first
Thanksgiving.

As soon as everyone was seated, Andrew, in his Sunday go-to-meeting best, gestured for them to join hands.
"Before we delve into all the tempting delicacies Frannie has prepared—with a little help from her sisters, I
might add—let's ask our Father-God to bless the food
and fellowship around the table."

After he had prayed, he picked up a terry-cloth bib
from beside his plate. "Don't forget your bibs, folks.
There's one for everybody. Don't be shy. Tie them on.

They'll protect your holiday duds. If you're as klutzy as I am, you may need two!''

He sat down, fastened his bib around his neck and smoothed it over his navy blazer. "Okay, folks, your turn." There was a titter of laughter around the table as everyone obliged.

Bree glanced over at Eric to see whether he considered their bib ritual tacky, but he was smiling broadly as he secured his over his blue dress shirt.

"Now, don't we all look stunning," said Cassie, with a playful toss of her honey-blond hair. She and Antonio had been married for just five months now, and Brianna had never seen her sister look happier or more at peace. She fairly glowed.

So did Antonio, with his bronze coloring and raven hair so much like his mother's. With a graceful flourish, he raised his goblet of sparkling cider and in his sonorous tenor declared, "Before we eat, I propose a toast. To the remarkable Rowlands clan and those who love them!"

Brianna stole another glance at Eric as she raised her glass and repeated the toast. *To the Rowlands clan and those who love them!* Eric said the words as willingly as did the others. *Those who love them.* Was it possible that he cared for her as much as she cared for him? She had no idea. As much as they both loved Charity, he still remained closemouthed about his feelings for her.

"Brianna, wake up and pass the gravy," said Frannie, her blue eyes flashing in her perfect, porcelain face. Her full, opalescent lips settled into a little pout. The youngest, she was used to having her own way. "Everyone's starving, girl. Keep the food moving, okay?"

Bree smiled, sheepish. "Sorry, sis, my mind wandered."

Frannie tucked her flowing amber hair behind one ear and lowered her thick lashes. "Well, considering how hard I worked on this dinner, I expect everyone to give it their undivided attention."

"We will, daughter, don't you worry." Andrew passed the turkey platter to Juliana. "It's heavy, Jewel. I'll hold it, while you spear yourself a leg or some white meat."

Juliana helped herself, then held the platter for her daughter. Belina, a slender girl with a delicate face and sable-black hair like her mother's, reached tentatively for the turkey. She was wearing a tea-rose jacquard dress that accented her fragile grace. "Everything looks delicious," she said in her soft, breathy voice.

Silently, Bree marveled at how far Belina had come both physically and emotionally since they had met last year. Since the car accident that had killed her father, Belina had spent half her life in a wheelchair, paralyzed and hiding a facial disfigurement resulting from the crash. In the past year, a vigorous regimen of physical therapy had enabled her to shed the wheelchair for a cane, and according to her doctors, soon even that would be unnecessary.

"You're looking wonderful, Belina," said Bree when their eyes met across the table.

The girl's face reddened and she lowered her gaze. She still wasn't fully at ease around others. "Thank you," she murmured softly.

"Yes, my daughter is beautiful!" agreed Juliana in her most buoyant voice. "I am so proud of her. She has healed from her recent surgery. She is taking classes at the university and doing very well. One of these days she won't need me anymore."

"Oh, Mama, I'll always need you."

"But not in the same way. You are becoming an independent woman."

"Yes, we all see the change in her," said Cassie. "We're thrilled with her progress."

"I think we're embarrassing her," said Antonio. "Maybe we should let my dear sister eat in peace."

"Speaking of eating, keep that food moving," urged Frannie. "Has everyone had the mashed potatoes? What about the stuffing? There's more of everything in the kitchen. And hot rolls in the oven."

"We're doing fine, doll baby," said her father with a hearty chuckle. "Eric, in case you haven't guessed by now, Frannie's our little mother hen. She's appointed herself a committee of one to supervise this family and make sure the household is humming along smoothly."

"Oh, Daddy, I'm not like that. I just pitch in where I'm needed. And since my sisters are a bit weak in the culinary department, that leaves me to make sure you eat well."

Andrew brandished a satisfied grin and patted his middle. "Oh, there's no question about my eating well, pumpkin."

"Actually, Cassandra has become quite a bon vivant," said Antonio with a playful wink. "A fine foods connoisseur in her own right, whenever Mother lets her in the kitchen."

"Now, Tonio, stop that," scolded Juliana. "Cassie can have the kitchen anytime she wishes."

"Your mother's right," said Cassie. "We do very well at sharing the kitchen."

"But who knows? Maybe one of these days I will bow out and let Cassandra take charge," said Juliana with a mysterious smile.

"Now, why would you do that, Mother, when we all get along so well together?" enquired Antonio.

Bree noticed a private glance pass between Juliana and her father. They were cooking up something, and it had nothing to do with the kitchen.

While Bree wondered what was brewing between her father and Juliana, Frannie slipped away to the kitchen and came back with a basket of hot rolls and more cranberry sauce. "Eat up, everybody. There's still a ton of food in the kitchen."

"Daughter, you always make enough food for thrashers."

"You always say that, Daddy," mused Frannie, "and to this day I can't figure out who the 'thrashers' are."

"Come to think of it, I haven't the slightest idea. It's just something my dad used to say."

"Well, I have something to say," said Frannie, giving her sister a knowing smile. "I want to know what has Cassie glowing so much. She looks positively radiant."

Antonio slipped his arm around his wife and whispered something in her ear.

"Okay, Tonio," warned Brianna, "no secrets around here."

Cassie folded her hands under her chin and smiled her inscrutable Mona Lisa smile. "All right, I cannot tell a lie."

"'Fess up," said Frannie. "You look like the cat that swallowed the canary."

"Not exactly," said Antonio with a sly chuckle.

Blushing roses colored Cassie's cheeks. She gazed around the room, her mirthful blue eyes sweeping each face. "The truth is...I'm pregnant."

"I knew it!" Frannie exclaimed with a triumphant little whoop.

Brianna drew back, stunned. Cassie? Having a baby? No, not now. Not so soon. She couldn't. Wouldn't! Not when Bree still didn't know whether she might lose her precious Charity.

Her father was already out of his chair and hugging Cassie. "Congratulations, darling. How about that! You're going to make me a grandpa!"

Bree watched in aching silence as everyone around the table heaped their praises and felicitations on a beaming Cassie. What was wrong with Bree that she felt no excitement and joy for her sister? Why wasn't she as jubilant as the rest of the family?

"Bree? Aren't you happy for me?"

Brianna shook off her reverie and flashed her most cheery smile. "Of course, Cassie. I…I'm thrilled. But I didn't realize you wanted to start a family so soon. You and Antonio are still practically honeymooners."

"And we will be honeymooners for years to come," said Antonio. "We will share our joy with our little bambino."

"I'm only two months along," said Cassie, "so it'll be a while. But we're very excited."

"Speaking of babies," said Brianna, "I think I hear Charity crying upstairs. She's probably wet and hungry."

"Well, bring her down and give her some turkey," quipped Frannie. "Or maybe some yams or green bean casserole."

"I think she'll be happy with formula," said Bree. She started to push back her chair, but Eric stopped her.

"I'll go get her. You finish eating."

"But you're not finished, either."

"No problem. I'll change her and bring her down, while you warm her bottle."

After Eric had headed upstairs, Cassie made a little clucking sound in her throat.

"What's that about?" asked Bree warily.

"Nothing at all, dear sister. It's just...well, you seem to have Eric well trained. He makes a wonderful daddy."

Brianna bristled. "What are you trying to say?"

Cassie examined her polished fingernails. "I'm just making an observation. Eric is devoted to that little girl."

"Yes, he is, but that's as far as it goes."

"Are you saying there's nothing going on between the two of you?" asked Frannie. "You can't make me believe that."

"It's the truth," said Bree. She hated having her family quiz her like this. Their suspicions put her on the defensive and made her stomach churn. "There's nothing going on in the romance department. We're just friends."

"Well, if you ask me," said her father with a twinkle in his eyes, "Eric Wingate is captivated by both Brianna and Charity."

"You're wrong, Daddy. Dead wrong." Before anyone could say another word, Bree got out of her chair and headed for the kitchen to warm Charity's bottle. A heavy ache spread through her chest like milk spilled on the floor; the hurt ran every which way, unstoppable.

She returned to the dining room with the warmed bottle, just as Eric came bounding into the room with a fussy Charity in his arms. Her blue eyes were wet with tears and her round cheeks were apple-red. Her little pink lips were blowing bubbles.

"Here's our girl!" Gently Eric placed the squirming baby in Brianna's arms.

Bree sat back down at the table, tested the bottle's warmth and nudged the rubber nipple into Charity's eager mouth.

"Just think," Cassie murmured to Antonio. "It won't be long before we have a darling little baby like that."

"I can't wait, sweetheart." Antonio turned his gaze to Brianna. "Tell me, what's happening with Charity? Are you still looking for adoptive parents?"

Bree cast a sidelong glance at Eric. Let him do the explaining.

"Actually, we've put our search on hold for the time being." Eric sounded a bit ill at ease, as if he hadn't reconciled the situation in his mind. "Brianna and I are considering other options. We both care a great deal for Charity, and we would both like to be part of her life. However, neither of us is in an optimal position to adopt her."

"So what are your alternatives?" asked Cassie.

"Well, to be candid, I'm seriously considering adopting Charity myself," said Eric. "She is my sister's child. And, of course, Brianna could have unlimited visitation."

Bree stared in astonishment at Eric. In all their time together, he had never come right out and said he was planning to adopt Charity. "You're really thinking of adopting her?" she said numbly.

Eric looked at her with a mixture of dismay and chagrin. "I didn't mean to blurt it out like that, Bree. But it has been on my mind for some time. But that doesn't mean you can't help raise her. I know how much you love her. I would never keep her from you. You're like a...a mother to her."

Hot tears smarted in Bree's eyes. "I'm the only mother she's ever known!" She drew in a shuddering breath. "You must realize, Eric, I've thought of adopting her, too."

Eric poked idly at his green beans. "Well, then, there's always…joint custody."

"Now it sounds like we're trying to work out the terms of a divorce!" Bree blinked back angry tears. What was wrong with Eric that he couldn't see what was staring him straight in the face? The solution wasn't single parenthood or joint custody. The three of them were meant to be a family! But being a family meant two parents who loved each other, and obviously the idea had never entered Eric's head. "Let's not discuss our problems here. This is supposed to be a pleasant Thanksgiving dinner."

"I'm sorry, Bree," said Cassie. "I didn't mean to—"

"No, it's okay. I'm fine. Everything's fine and dandy."

Eric reached over and patted her arm, then squeezed Charity's crocheted booty. "I apologize, Bree. I didn't mean to blurt out my thoughts about adopting—"

"No, I said it's okay. Let's just drop it and enjoy our dinner." Charity was nursing languidly, so Bree joggled the bottle to rouse her. Charity's eyes flew open, and, sensing Bree's tension, she wriggled in her arms and started fussing.

Bree shoved back her chair and announced, "I'm going to feed Charity upstairs. There's too much commotion down here."

Brianna hurried out of the room with the whimpering baby before anyone could stop her or guess the real reason for her unceremonious retreat. The last thing she wanted was the humiliation of everyone guessing how much she cared for Eric and how little he cared for her. Most of all, Eric must never know what a lovesick fool she was.

But just when she thought her secret was safe and she was home free, she heard Eric's footsteps behind her on the stairs, and his voice calling, "Bree, wait up. Please, don't be upset!"

Not looking back, she took long strides down the hall to the nursery. Once inside the cozy, pastel room, she laid Charity in her crib and tucked a soft velour blanket around her.

Eric entered quietly, his bib still in place over his starched blue dress shirt. "Bree, are you okay?"

"Fine." She frowned at him. "You look like a penguin."

"So do you."

They both pulled off their bibs and tossed them on the changing table. Eric's gaze swept approvingly over her mint-green angora sweater and short pleated skirt. His thick hair was mussed, a wayward curl inching over his wide forehead. His dark brows shadowed his shrewd eyes.

"What's going on here, Bree?" he asked, lightly placing his hands on her shoulders. "Why did you leave the table? Why are you putting Charity down, when she hasn't even finished her bottle?"

Bree looked away, lest he see her tears, and covered her quivering lips with her hand. "I...I don't know."

"Is it about me adopting Charity?"

She forced herself to meet his gaze. "You never mentioned it before."

He tightened his grip on her arms. "I'm sorry, Bree. The words just sort of popped out. Heaven knows, we've been going along in limbo long enough. But I would never do anything you wouldn't approve of. If you're worried about my parents raising Charity, I want to assure you—"

"No, that's not it." The tears were gathering like a raging flood behind her eyes. She couldn't hold them back much longer.

"Then, tell me, Bree! Don't keep me guessing!"

"I can't!" A large tear streamed down her cheek.

Eric looked alarmed. "Don't cry, Bree. I won't adopt Charity without your approval. I promise. Just don't cry. I can't bear to see you cry."

"I'm not crying," she choked miserably.

"Just tell me what you want," he urged. "Maybe we can work out the joint custody thing. It's irregular, but possible."

"No, no, no!" The torrent inside her broke in great, gulping sobs.

For an instant Eric seemed stunned, unsure how to react. After a moment, he gathered her into his arms and held her head against his chest, letting her cry it out. "There, there," he murmured, like a father comforting his child. "It's okay, dear Brianna. Don't cry. You're going to be okay."

"No, I'm not," she mumbled against his strapping chest.

He combed his fingers through her hair and massaged the back of her neck. "Tell me. Please. What has you hurting like this?"

She looked up at him with glistening eyes and a tear-stained face. His eyes searched hers with sympathy and concern. She parted her lips as if to speak, but no words came. She was drowning in the infinite depth of his eyes, her heart aching with love she could never reveal. She couldn't tear her gaze from his.

The moment seemed to swell into something timeless and eternal, as if they were no longer mere mortals standing in a baby's nursery on Thanksgiving Day. They could have been anywhere on earth, or nowhere, or part of the heavens, or in a dimension beyond time and space. She was aware of only one preeminent fact. Eric Wingate was gathering her into his arms, his face so close that his tangy breath warmed her cheek as he kissed her salty tears, one by one. And now his eager lips were upon hers, moving with exquisite tenderness.

Bree yielded readily to his embrace, and, as the kiss deepened, she returned it.

Within moments—or was it an eternity?—Eric released her and stepped back, his expression stricken. "I'm sorry, Brianna. I didn't mean to do that. Forgive me." He lifted his palms placatingly and took another step backward. "I don't know what got into me. We're in enough of a dilemma here without getting into a foolish emotional entanglement."

"Foolish?" she echoed, her mind reeling. Dazed and bewildered, she touched her mouth; she could still feel the sweet pressure of Eric's lips. His kiss had been the most deliciously sublime moment of her life, and Eric was calling it *foolish?*

He paced the floor, rubbing his hands together with a restless energy. "I hope you can forget this, Brianna. I swear it'll never happen again. If we're ever going to resolve this situation with Charity, we've got to keep our heads. If we rush off on some emotional tangent, we could mess things up for all three of us."

"You're right." Bree said the words in a solemn monotone, not because she believed them but because she knew that was what Eric expected to hear.

After a minute she drifted over to the crib, gripped

the oak rail with both hands and gazed down at her precious Charity. The baby's eyes were half closed, and she was sucking noisily on her fist. She looked so peaceful and content, as if she knew instinctively that everything would turn out right somehow.

But Brianna couldn't promise that. At this moment she had no idea in which direction her own life, let alone Charity's, was moving. The future loomed as a dark, ominous cloud ready to envelop them all. She could lose Charity and Eric, and neither of them would ever know the enormity of her loss. As suddenly as Bree's hopes had been raised, they had been violently dashed—all by a man who hadn't the slightest idea how she felt…and obviously didn't care.

"You are all right, aren't you, Brianna?" Eric repeated, a rumble of urgency in his deep voice. "Man, I feel like such a fool—a total jerk—taking liberties with someone I respect so much. I was wrong, Bree. Tell me we can still be friends."

She started to speak, but her mouth was dry, a bruised, salty sensation on her lips now. She tried again, but her throat closed over the words.

"I don't blame you if you don't trust me," he rushed on with a remorseful agitation. "All I can say, Bree, is I'll never take advantage of you like that again."

She pivoted and faced him, scouring her mind for some way to tell him his kiss was exactly what she wanted, what she longed for, what she craved. But to confess such neediness would risk her losing his respect forever.

"It's okay," she mumbled dispiritedly. "It's forgotten."

The relief on Eric's face was enormous, but before he could reply, a knock sounded on the nursery door.

After a moment Frannie peeked inside and said, "Hey, sis, I'm sorry to interrupt."

Brianna forced a smile and said with as much nonchalance as she could muster, "You weren't interrupting, Frannie. Come in."

Frannie stepped inside, an odd expression playing on her lips. Worry? Concern? Uncertainty?

"What's wrong, Frannie? A problem downstairs?"

"I'm not sure."

Brianna felt a bristling tension along her backbone, the sensation of hair-raising alarm; she felt like a cat arching its back when it senses danger. "Tell me, Fran. What's going on?"

"There's someone at the door to see you."

Bree glanced fleetingly at Eric. "Who is it?"

"He didn't give his name, but..." Frannie looked apprehensively from Eric to Brianna. "He says to tell you..." Her words hung in the air like a death knell. "He says he's Charity's father."

Chapter Thirteen

Sam Dillard stood in the foyer in baggy jeans and a beige polo shirt. He was a tall, lanky, ruddy-faced youth with a mop of curly blond hair the color of beach sand and the hint of a flaxen beard on his narrow jaw. With pale blue eyes, ashen brows and a wide, chiseled mouth that seemed permanently drawn into a sneer, he looked like a stereotypical Southern California beach bum.

As Brianna approached him, she tried to generate a smile, but the best she could manage was a tight grimace. "Hello," she said tentatively, holding out her hand. An odd childlike quality in the youth's face blended with a smoldering insolence. He didn't bother to shake her hand.

"I'm Sam Dillard," he announced, almost as if he dared Bree to challenge him.

Eric stepped forward and held out his hand, too, and waited until the boy grudgingly accepted. In a sonorous voice that hinted only slightly of wariness and skepticism, Eric said, "I'm Eric Wingate. Marnie's brother."

The youth nodded. "Yeah, Marnie used to talk about you. Said you were one cool dude."

"And this is Brianna Rowlands," Eric continued. "I assume you know Marnie stayed here in her home until she had her baby."

Sam glanced around with a gaze that was part defiance, part admiration. "Yeah, Marnie liked it here. A lot. A whole lot."

"We were just finishing dinner," said Bree, with a nod toward the dining room. "Would you like to join us for dessert?"

He shrank back. "Naw, I already ate. I'm not here to socialize. I probably shouldn't have come today, this being Thanksgiving and all, but I figured at least you'd be home."

"What can we do for you, Sam?" asked Eric in a businesslike voice.

An unexpected gentleness flickered in the boy's sea-blue eyes. "I just came to see my little girl."

The words tore at Brianna's heart. His little girl? What right did he have to call Charity his little girl? "You want to see Charity? Why...why now?"

Sam's eyes darkened and his brow furrowed. "Why not? She's my daughter. I have a right."

Eric broke in. "As I understand it, Sam, you surrendered your parental rights. We have the document with your signature."

Sam shifted uneasily from one foot to the other. "Yeah, I signed the paper, but my lawyer says there's a period of time before it's official. In case I change my mind."

"Is that what you're doing?" asked Bree, her breath catching in her chest like a cord knotted too tightly. "Are you saying you want Charity?"

Sam shoved his long fingers through his curls. They flowed back from his forehead in rolling, sunlit waves.

What most women wouldn't give for a head of hair like that, thought Bree.

"What about it, Sam?" prodded Eric. "Are you telling us you want custody of your daughter?"

He shrugged. "I don't know. Maybe. Maybe not. I haven't even seen my kid yet, so how do I know what I want?"

Bree glanced at Eric as if to ask, *What do we do? Do we let him see her or send him on his way?*

Eric took the lead. "Sure, you can see her, Sam— but she's sleeping right now."

"That's okay. I'll wait."

Fighting the panic rising in her chest, Bree gestured toward the living room. "All right. Would you like to come sit down?"

Now that he knew he wouldn't get an argument, Sam seemed more relaxed and accommodating. "Sure, if it's no trouble. You guys go on with your dinner."

Bree led Sam into the living room. "My sister's probably serving dessert now. Are you sure you wouldn't like a piece of homemade pumpkin pie?"

Sam sat down on the sofa, his long legs sprawling out like awkward stilts, the flicker of a smile lighting his pale eyes. "Um, now that you mention it, pumpkin pie is my favorite."

"Fine. I'll get us some. I'm sure the others won't mind if we have our pie here."

"I'll help," said Eric, nudging Bree. "Would you like something to drink, Sam? Coffee? Tea?"

"A soda, if you've got it."

"I'm sure we'll find some. We'll be right back."

As Eric ushered Bree through the dining room to the

kitchen, she flashed him a beseeching glance, as if to say, *What now? How do we handle this?*

His returning glance said, *Just hold on. Don't panic. We'll manage somehow.*

Frannie was in the kitchen cutting the pie, when Brianna burst in, breathless, her heart pounding. She seized her sister's arm and said urgently, "Frannie, you were right. The boy at the door is Charity's father. What are we going to do? What if he wants to take her away from us?"

Frannie's gaze moved worriedly from Bree to Eric. "He can't, can he? Didn't he give up his rights?"

A tendon tightened in Eric's jaw. "There's a period of time before it's official. Until then, he could nullify the document and petition the court for custody."

Bree clasped her hands to her mouth. "Oh, Eric! Would they automatically give him custody?"

"No, Bree, they wouldn't." Eric squeezed her shoulder reassuringly. "If other parties wanted to adopt Charity, they could petition the court, and there would be a hearing to determine the most suitable home for her. The judge would make the final decision."

Bree was trembling now, near tears. "That boy can't just waltz back into her life now and take her away from us. He didn't even want her. He wanted Marnie to get an abortion."

"Maybe he just wants to see her one time before it's final," said Frannie. "Maybe he'll just take a look at her, be satisfied, and go on his way."

"No, that's too easy. He wants more, I can feel it."

Eric picked up two slices of pie. "Well, for now, we'll take him some pie and soda and humor him."

"Frannie, tell Daddy what's happening," said Bree.

"We'll have our pie in the living room with Sam. Be praying, okay?"

Frannie handed Bree another slice, several napkins and silverware. "Here you go. I'll bring some coffee, if you like."

"Soda for Sam," said Eric.

They settled around the coffee table, Sam and Brianna on the sofa, Eric in the overstuffed chair.

"Boy, this is good!" Sam exclaimed after he had sampled his pie. "Someone around here is an awesome cook."

"My sister," said Bree. "She's the best."

"I heard that," said Frannie in her most musical voice. She breezed into the room with the soda and two coffees, and set them on the table. Bree started to make introductions, but Frannie headed her off. "Sam and I already met at the door, remember?"

Sam looked up at Frannie and winked. "If I'd known you could cook like this, I'd have lied about already eating."

Frannie smiled and tossed back her amber hair. "That's okay. There's more turkey and stuffing in the kitchen."

"Thanks, anyway. I like the pie."

"There's more of that in the kitchen, too. We don't frown on second helpings around here."

"Yeah? I'll keep that in mind." Sam's smile lit up his whole face. Bree could see that he was taken with Frannie. Already he seemed more relaxed and approachable.

After Frannie had returned to the kitchen, they focused on their dessert, as if this were an ordinary guest paying a routine visit. Finally Eric broke the silence. "Sam, I suppose you know Marnie never told our family about you. My parents and I didn't even know about the baby until after Marnie had died. Now that we have a chance, I'd like to get acquainted.''

"Yeah, sure.'' Sam turned his glass of soda between his palms. "So what do you want to know?''

"Anything you can tell us,'' said Bree.

"Not much to tell. I'm twenty. Just finished my sophomore year at San Diego State. Majoring in computer science. I live with my mom and stepdad in Pacific Beach. I got a neat little sports car I'll be making payments on till I'm fifty. And I...I made the biggest mistake of my life when I let Marnie go.''

"Then, why did you, Sam? We just want to understand what happened,'' said Bree, searching for words. "We loved Marnie very much, and we know she loved you.''

"I loved her, too,'' said Sam in a nearly inaudible voice. "I should have gone to her funeral, but I figured I was the last person anybody wanted to see.''

"You could have come,'' said Eric. "I can't speak for my parents, but I wouldn't have had a problem with it.''

Sam sat forward, leaning his elbows on his knees, and shook his head solemnly. "I can't believe she's gone.''

"Me, neither,'' said Eric with a catch in his voice.

"I didn't know her for long,'' said Bree, "but we loved each other like sisters.''

Sam looked up, his eyes glistening. Varying shades of emotion played out in his face, like shifting sands under the surface of his skin—love, regret, anger, guilt—subtly changing his features.

"She wanted that baby. I tried to talk her into an abortion, but man, she wouldn't budge. I told her we were through if she didn't get rid of it. I mean, what were we going to do with a baby, with both of us in school? But she was gonna have that kid if it killed her—'' A sob broke from his lips. "And I guess it did.''

The room rang with an awkward silence until Bree spoke up. "Marnie loved that baby more than her own life. That's why it's so important to Eric and me that Charity have the best home possible, a loving family, a good future.''

Sam brushed self-consciously at one eye. "That's what I want for her, too. She's my kid. She deserves the best.''

"And what is that, Sam?'' asked Eric. "What do you consider best for your daughter?''

He shrugged. "I don't know. I guess that's what I'm here to find out.''

As if on cue, Bree heard Charity crying upstairs—a soft, plaintive cry that would soon escalate to an insistent wail. Her heart sank. Somehow, she had hoped to avoid this unplanned encounter between father and daughter. But there was no escaping it now. She would just have to steel herself and endure it. And pray that once Sam had seen his child, he would withdraw from her life forever.

"Looks like Charity's awake,'' she said through tight lips. "I'll go change her and bring her downstairs.''

Sam jumped up and rubbed his hands together nervously. "Do you need help? I won't volunteer for diaper duty, but I could rock her or sing to her or something.''

With a heavy sigh, Bree got up and headed for the stairs. "No, Sam. I'll go get her. You can hold her down here.''

Sam sat back down and rubbed his palms on his

knees, as if to dry them. "Guess I'm ready as I'll ever be to see my little girl."

As Brianna ascended the stairs and walked down the hall to the nursery, she wrestled with her emotions…and prayed. *Dear Father, please don't let this be happening. Don't let this stranger, this man who broke Marnie's heart, come and take away our little girl. She belongs to Eric and me, even if the two of us can never be more than friends. Please, Father! Minutes ago I was afraid of losing Eric. Now it looks like I could lose Charity, too!*

Bree's anxieties grew as she changed Charity and dressed her in a frilly pink dress and lacy booties. "You look so pretty, little girl," she murmured, stroking her cheek. "Part of me wants you to look nice for your daddy—part of me wants to run away and never let him see you. What if he falls in love with you like I have?"

Charity wiggled her chubby arms and legs and made a gurgling sound that showed on her rosy lips as half smile, half bubble. With an aching heart, Bree scooped the baby up and carried her downstairs. "Here she is— our dry, happy little girl," she said brightly as she rocked Charity in her arms.

Sam jumped up from the sofa, all awkward arms and legs, and stumbled over to Brianna, an expression of pure astonishment on his face. His blue eyes grew round as china plates. "Wow! She's so little!"

"She's just right for her age," said Bree, swallowing over her fear. "Almost three months old."

Sam gingerly extended his fingertips and touched Charity's cheek. She fastened her wide blue eyes on him and made a little *aaaahhh* sound.

"Man, look, she's talking to me." He grew bolder and gently knuckled her rosy cheek. "Hey, little girl,

I'm your daddy. Bet you didn't think you were going to see me today, did you? You're just about the prettiest little thing I ever did see. Got your mama's eyes and nose and my curly blond hair.''

"Do you want to hold her?" asked Bree, praying he wouldn't.

Sam took a backward step. "Um, I don't know about that. I never held a baby. Looks to me like she could break real easy. I wouldn't want to drop her."

Eric got up and came over and put a coaxing hand on Sam's shoulder. Bree could see that he was chomping at the bit to get rid of the boy. "Well, you've seen her now, Sam, so maybe it's time for you to—"

Sam turned sharply and faced Eric with fire in his ice-blue eyes. "Hold on, man. I just got here. Give me some time with my little girl, okay?"

Bree broke in quickly, before the situation deteriorated beyond repair. "That's fine, Sam. Stay as long as you like. There's no hurry. Why don't you sit down on the sofa, and I'll put Charity in your arms? That way, you don't have to worry about dropping her."

As Sam turned his attention back to his tiny daughter, his features softened and he evinced that little-boy naiveté again. "Okay, sure. That's a good idea. I should hold her. I don't want her growing up thinking her daddy never held her."

He sat down and held his arms out clumsily, as Brianna handed him the baby. "There, that's it," she said softly. "Support her neck. Babies this young can't hold their heads up yet."

With a frown of concentration, Sam shifted Charity in his arms, tipping her one way and then the other. "Man, she's so soft and wobbly. And light. Like JELL-O. You sure she's okay?"

"You're doing fine," said Bree, sitting down beside him.

Eric sat on the other side. "She likes to be held a little more upright, Sam, so she can see things around her. If you hold her lying flat, she thinks she's going to be fed, and if you don't stick a bottle in her mouth, she'll start shrieking. And she can break the sound barrier with her cries."

"Man, I don't want that. No crying. I can't stand to hear a baby cry."

"All babies cry, Sam," said Bree. "It's their only way to let people know they need something—milk, warmth, a clean diaper..."

"Sometimes Charity cries when she has gas on her stomach. She has a real touchy tummy. Cries with colic sometimes. Or her cries may mean she hasn't been burped enough."

Sam bounced her tentatively against his chest. "How do you ever figure out what she needs?"

"It takes time," said Bree. "Eric and I have learned her needs by spending time with her. Getting to know her."

"She looks happy. I guess you've been doing it right." Sam paused for a moment, his expression growing somber. "Have you found a family to adopt her?"

"Not yet," said Eric. "We've interviewed a number of couples, but we haven't found the right family yet."

"I guess that's best," said Sam. "Seeing as how I'm not sure yet what I want to do."

Eric cleared his throat uneasily. "You demonstrated what you wanted to do when you signed off your rights, Sam."

"Yeah, I know, but like I said, I've still got time to change my mind. Right?"

"Theoretically, yes. But the sooner Charity's future is settled, the better for her."

"Then, how come you haven't found a family for her yet? Her new parents are going to have to learn all the things about her you already know."

Brianna and Eric exchanged troubled glances. Sam was right. He had innocently pinpointed the very issue they had been dancing around for months. What to do about Charity. Who would be given the privilege and joy of raising her?

Lord, let it be me! Bree prayed silently. *No one knows it yet, but I can't give her up. To anyone! Ever!*

Chapter Fourteen

Christmas was in the air, the earth resplendent with colored lights and candy canes and silver stars. The air filled with carols and cantatas. The hustle and bustle of eager shoppers, and foil-wrapped packages heaped under popcorn-strung trees. The overhanging mistletoe and circling wreaths. The shops festooned with Santas and sleighs and bright banners with holiday greetings.

But Brianna couldn't feel it.

Couldn't summon a modicum of holiday spirit.

Not when her own spirits were sinking to new depths of melancholy and gloom.

Eric had just phoned with the news that she had been dreading for weeks. Sam Dillard had petitioned the court for custody of Charity. His parents were supporting him in the endeavor. It looked like Charity might be going home with her daddy, after all.

Bree should have seen it coming. During the past few weeks Sam and his parents had visited Charity several times, and each time Bree had seen Sam bonding more and more with his tiny daughter. They were a nice enough family, the Dillards—Sam, his mother and step-father. In fact, try as she might, Bree couldn't make herself dislike them. Even Sam. For all his mistakes with Marnie, he seemed to be trying to redeem himself now.

But for Bree, even the perfect parents wouldn't be good enough for Charity. There were only two people she wanted to see raising Marnie's little girl, and even that prospect seemed impossible at this point. Since Thanksgiving, she and Eric had made no noticeable headway in their relationship. So if Charity was to have a real family, it would be the Dillards by default.

"Anyway, that's the scoop," said Eric over the phone. "Sam wants his daughter, and his folks are backing him all the way."

"Eric, what can we do?"

"We need to talk about it, Bree. Tonight."

"I'll put Charity to bed about seven. Come over then."

"Fine. Keep her up till I get there. I'd like to kiss her good-night."

Eric arrived just before seven that brisk, starry mid-December evening. His expression was somber as he climbed the stairs to the nursery. But a smile broke on his lips as he lifted Charity out of her crib. "How's my beautiful little girl?" he said in the lyrical falsetto he used whenever he talked to her. "You're my darling little dumpling girl, aren't you?"

Charity cooed and grinned and blew bubbles. She flapped her plump arms and kicked her pudgy legs.

"Goodness, Eric, she's sure excited to see you."

"Not half as happy as I am to see her." He bounced her and rocked her and talked more baby talk for several minutes, while Bree watched with a wistful smile. She loved the way the two interacted. It was obvious they were crazy about each other.

Finally Eric laid a drowsy Charity back in her bed and tucked her favorite blanket around her. Bree turned off the light, and they tiptoed out the door and returned downstairs to the living room.

"Where is everyone?" asked Eric.

"Daddy's at a deacons' meeting and Frannie's teaching an art class."

"So it's just us?"

"Just us."

They sat down together on the sofa facing the bay window, which framed the huge blue spruce trimmed with angel hair and delicate Victorian ornaments. Except for the blinking white lights on the tree, only a single table lamp cast a golden glow over the large, comfortable room. The air was fragrant with pine needles, tree sap and a tangy Christmas potpourri. Earlier, Bree had put on some easy-listening music, and now a fifties ballad was playing on the CD player.

"Would you like something to drink? Coffee? Hot chocolate?"

"No, I'm fine for now." Eric unbuttoned his sport coat and loosened his tie. "But go ahead if you'd like."

"Maybe later." Bree sensed that he had something more to tell her about the custody case. She prayed it would be good news. "Have you learned any more since this afternoon?"

"Not exactly, but I wanted to fill you in on the details."

"Did you talk directly with the Dillards?"

"At first their lawyer called and told me they were petitioning the court for custody. Then, a little later, Mrs. Dillard phoned. I think because I'm Marnie's brother, she wanted me to understand where they're coming from.''

"What did she say?''

"She was quite pleasant. From what I've seen she's a reasonable, intelligent woman. She said their family had been trying to decide what to do for a long time, and they didn't want to take any action until they were sure Sam was serious about being Charity's father. Not just when he felt like it, but on a consistent, day-to-day basis.''

"And he's ready now?''

"So he says.''

"How can he know something like that? He's not around her every day, feeding and bathing and changing her. He just sees her when she's dressed up for him. He plays with her for a little while and then goes home. He has no idea what it's like to take care of a baby twenty-four hours a day, seven days a week.''

"No, he doesn't. And I don't see how he could handle it while going to school, working part time and trying to maintain some kind of social life.''

"Can't we reason with him?''

"He wouldn't believe us. He'd suspect our motives. And I'm afraid he'd dig his heels in deeper. That's how it looks to me.''

"Then, we're going to lose her, aren't we.'' Bree covered her mouth with her hand as if to stop a wave of nausea churning in her stomach. "Oh, Eric, after all these months of loving her, we're going to have to let her go.''

He slipped his arm around the back of the sofa and lightly massaged her shoulder. "Not necessarily, Bree.''

"But what can we do?''

He said the words quietly and precisely. "We can

petition the court for custody, too, and let a judge decide who will be the better parents.''

She stared at him. They had talked about this before, in theory, but it had been mere conjecture. Now he sounded dead serious. ''You mean the two of us...adopt Charity?''

''Yes, us. Adopt her. Why not, Bree?'' As Eric's voice rose with fervor, his fingers kneaded her shoulder until she winced. ''What do you say? We love her as much as any two parents could.''

''But we both agreed she needs a real home. A family.''

''Yes, I know...''

''A mother and a father. Not two single parents.''

''Yes, you're right.'' Eric's deep chestnut eyes kindled with excitement. ''You're absolutely right, Bree. Every word you say. That's why...I've thought about it and prayed about it and I can think of only one solution.''

She held her breath, her heart pausing in mid-beat, waiting.

In his most resonant voice he said, ''I want you to marry me, Brianna.''

The magic words. Incredible. Had he actually said them, or was it a trick of her imagination? She struggled to find her voice. ''What did you say?''

Eric seized her hands and held them like little doves between his palms. ''I'm not very good at this, Bree. I'm saying this all wrong, but, as I see it, it's the only choice we have, if we want to keep our little girl. Say you'll marry me.''

''Marry you?'' Bree repeated. Her mind was spinning dizzily, like a fanciful whirling dervish. She couldn't gather her thoughts or articulate the words. She could summon only one delicious, astonishing fact: He loves me! He actually loves me!

"You don't have to give me an answer right now," he said as he pressed her hands against his chest. "I know it's a surprise. I'm coming out of left field with this, but I've racked my brain for another tactic, and I keep coming up empty-handed."

Slowly Brianna withdrew her hands. Something in Eric's tone, in his words, wasn't ringing true. There was something missing, something askew. "Just what are you saying, Eric?"

"I told you I'm not good at this, Bree." He ran his fingers through his hair, mussing it, leaving little curls grazing his forehead. A sweet, boyish gesture, but something about it irritated Bree. Eric didn't look like a man hopelessly in love.

"Just tell me what you have in mind," she urged. "You say you want us to get married?"

He drummed his fingers on the back of the couch. "It wouldn't be a real marriage, of course. I wouldn't ask that of you, Brianna. But people get married for lots of reasons. Not just love." He chuckled mirthlessly. "In the old days marriages were arranged by one's parents. Sometimes complete strangers were joined in holy wedlock. At least we know each other. We're friends. Good friends, wouldn't you say?"

The giddy, reeling sensation in Brianna's head metamorphosed suddenly into a jarring, jolting, horrifying downward spiral. It felt as if her heart had hit rock bottom, unleashing a deluge of pain through her breast. She inhaled sharply, but couldn't catch her breath.

"Oh, Eric," she managed to say but no other words came.

He looked nonplussed, discomfited. His mouth tightened, and shadows formed around his eyes. "I can see I've shocked you. I shouldn't have put it that way. I know I'm asking a lot, maybe too much. After all, someday you'll want a real husband and children of your own. So I'll understand if you say no."

She found her voice at last. "I'm not saying no."

Eric's sturdy, aristocratic face brightened. "You're not?"

She shook her head as if to clear it. "I'm confused, Eric. I need to know more."

"Of course. Just ask."

She massaged her knuckles. Her hands felt stiff, clammy. "Are you saying you want us to enter into a loveless marriage? A marriage of convenience, for Charity's sake?"

"Yes, that's about it. We probably wouldn't stand a chance of adopting her as two single parents. But together, as husband and wife, we could offer her a traditional family. Of course, it would mean real sacrifice for both of us."

"And you're willing to...to sacrifice your life by marrying me?" she asked thickly.

Eric's dark brows knitted together in a perplexed *V*. "I wouldn't put it quite that way, Brianna. I think we could have a pleasant life together, raising Charity, supporting and encouraging one another. We already have real affection for each other, and I trust that would deepen over the years."

"Into what? Genuine...fondness?"

"Yes. Exactly."

Mortified, Brianna sank back weakly against the sofa pillows. *Dear God, this can't be happening. All my hopes and dreams dissolving into a ghastly nightmare. Like one appalling practical joke!*

"You know, Bree, we wouldn't have to have a fancy wedding. Just a simple ceremony with our families." Eric's voice resounded persuasively in the silent house. "Your father could officiate. And I have some money saved. We could put a down payment on a little house in the country, maybe even near Julian. You loved that little mining town, remember? It would be a good life, Bree. I'd do my best to make you happy. I make a respectable income. You could have anything you wanted."

Brianna couldn't respond. Her heart felt like stone. Her mind was still swirling in a vortex of pain and disappointment. Oh, Eric, Eric! she wailed silently. You say you could give me anything I want. Anything except what I crave the most.

Your love!

Chapter Fifteen

For Brianna, the next few days were like a reel of videotape playing on fast-forward—everything moving too quickly, hectic, unreal, the fleeting images a dizzying, exhausting blur. How had it happened that she found herself swept up in a series of bizarre circumstances beyond her control?

Sometime during the evening of Eric's improbable and devastating marriage proposal, she must have said yes. In her shock and dismay over the idea of a loveless marriage, she had acquiesced. Numbly, she had agreed to become Eric's wife so they stood a chance in court of winning custody of Charity.

And from that night on she was forced to live the deception, the travesty of an engagement Eric had instigated. She hated him for it, and yet loved him more than ever as they went through the motions of being a loving couple planning a lifetime together.

What hurt the most was the excitement she saw in her father's and sisters' faces when Eric made the official announcement at a family dinner the following

Sunday. The sparkle in their eyes was enough to light a small city. One by one they got up from the table and came around and hugged her and Eric, bubbling over with exclamations of joy.

"We knew it was just a matter of time, didn't we, sis?" whispered Frannie as they embraced. "You two were made for each other, and I'm so glad he finally had the smarts to see it."

"I pray you'll be as happy as Tonio and me," said Cassie, kissing her cheek. "Let me know if you need some pointers on picking out wedding gowns, florists and caterers. It can be overwhelming."

Bree nodded distractedly, but the only thing overwhelming at the moment was trying to keep up the pretense that she and Eric were like any other engaged couple.

Fooling her father was hardest of all. He swept her up in his arms and said with tears in his eyes, "I couldn't be happier, Bree. This is what I've been praying for for you, my darling daughter…to have a family of your own, a loving husband and a beautiful little girl."

"Thanks, Daddy," she whispered, then burst into tears.

He patted her tenderly. "You go ahead and cry, honey. I know those are tears of joy."

But there was little joy in Brianna's heart as she and Eric began making wedding plans and looking at model homes. She went along with whatever he suggested, because he had enough excitement for both of them. But it was as if all the energy and enthusiasm had been drained out of her at the prospect of facing a chaste and loveless future with a man she cherished so deeply.

Each landmark in their relationship that brought pleasure to Eric only made Bree feel more trapped and confused. First, there was his petition to the court to adopt Charity, specifying that they would be a married couple by the time of the adoption. The court case was set for late February. That meant they must be married in less than three months. As much as Bree wanted Charity for her own, she couldn't help thinking grudgingly, *So little time to arrange our farce of a wedding, or to prepare emotionally for this mockery of a marriage!*

The second landmark was Brianna's visit to the Wingate home to have Christmas Eve dinner with her future in-laws. Brianna had met Vivian and Edward Wingate the day she and Eric broke the news to them of their daughter's death. She had seen them again at Marnie's funeral. But never before had she encountered a couple who manifested such coldness, aloofness and indifference.

Eric wanted his parents not only to get to know Brianna but to meet their little granddaughter, Charity, as well. But Bree sensed from the moment she stepped through the door of the Wingate mansion that their goodwill efforts were doomed.

Edward Wingate showed them into the living room, an elegant, pristine room that looked anything but lived in. With its Victorian-style love seat and sofa, cherry wood tables and Queen Anne chairs, and plush ivory carpet and velour draperies, it could have been a room in one of the model homes she and Eric had visited recently.

Centered before the plate-glass window was the only sign of warmth and hominess—an artificial silver Christmas tree with gold bulbs and twinkling lights. Even the few gifts under the tree were wrapped in plain gold foil with silver bows and were fastidiously arranged.

"Your mother's in the kitchen working on dinner." Edward Wingate was a tall, broad-shouldered man with a barrel chest and an imposing, professorial air that kept others at a distance. His robust features were larger than life—a high forehead, beaklike nose, powerful jaw, and neatly trimmed white hair and beard. "Sit down and relax, son. You, too, Miss Rowlands. It'll be a few minutes."

"Thank you," said Bree. Edward's small, riveting brown eyes made her feel as if he could bore right through her and read her thoughts. Already she felt unnerved. What if Eric's parents refused to accept their engagement? What if they still wanted nothing to do with their tiny granddaughter? Would Eric suffer even greater estrangement from them?

Eric held out the infant carrier so that his father could catch a glimpse of Charity. "Father, don't you want to see your new granddaughter?"

Edward cast a wary glance at the sleeping infant bundled in pink blankets. "Sure, I want to see her, but I hate to disturb her now. I'll wait for your mother. We'll see her together."

Eric set the infant carrier on the floor beside the sofa. "Sure, Dad."

Bree winced at the disappointment in Eric's voice. "It's really okay, Mr. Wingate," she said quickly. "Charity's been asleep for hours. She needs to eat now, anyway, and I know she'd love to meet her grandfather."

"I said I'll wait."

The gruffness in his tone made Bree take a step backward. This was going to be harder than she'd expected.

"Like I said, son, sit down. I'll get your mother."

As Edward lumbered off down the hall, Bree and Eric sat down on the sofa and exchanged sympathetic glances.

Eric rubbed the back of his head. Bree could see the tension and frustration in his edgy demeanor as he muttered, "Maybe we shouldn't have come."

"We have to face them sometime. What better time than Christmas Eve?" Bree sounded more optimistic than she felt. If she had her way, she'd be walking out the door right now. But these were people Eric loved and needed in his life. His parents. Somehow she had to make the best of it.

Eric reached over and squeezed her hand. "It'll be okay, Bree. I promise."

She looked dubiously at him. "What do you think they'll say when they find out we're engaged?"

"I hope they'll be happy for us. As happy as I am."

For a moment she thought, He does care for me. He's saying I make him happy. Or did he mean she made him happy because she was enabling him to adopt Charity?

Bree heard someone approaching, and looked up to see Vivian Wingate—a slim, stylish matron in a blue pinstriped shirtdress, her salt-and-pepper hair tied back in an elegant twist. At first glance she was attractive, but then Bree saw the brittle tautness in her face, a disquieting tension. Her classic features seemed a bit too perfect, too intractably rigid—the high arch of her penciled brows, the austere line of her meticulously drawn lips, the vermilion rouge accenting her narrow cheekbones. It could all be a mask, mused Bree, the impeccable face camouflaging a hurting, needy woman Vivian wanted no one to see.

Vivian greeted Bree with a restrained smile. "How nice to see you again, Miss Rowlands."

"Thank you, Mrs. Wingate. It's good to see you again, too."

"Hello, Mother." Eric took her into his arms. "Merry Christmas."

"I'm not sure how merry it's going to be, son. Our first year without Marnie."

"At least we have Marnie's little girl." Eric nodded toward the sleeping baby in the carrier. "I've wanted you to meet your little granddaughter for a long time now." He stooped down, unfastened the clasp and lifted the bundled infant into his arms. "See, Mom? Doesn't she look like Marnie when she was a baby?"

Tears gathered in Vivian's eyes, but she kept her lips tightly drawn as she stepped back and touched her husband's arm. "Don't wake the poor little thing now, Eric. We're just about to sit down to dinner."

Eric stepped closer to his mother and pulled the blanket away from Charity's face. "Look at her, Mother. Your granddaughter. Isn't she beautiful? Can't you see Marnie in her?"

Vivian lifted tentative fingers toward the baby, then let her hand fall to her side. "Oh, Eric, darling, you know babies at this age all look alike."

"Why did you bring her here, son?" His father stepped forward and slipped a protective arm around his wife. "Don't you see what it's doing to your mother?"

Eric's face reddened with vexation. "What am I doing?" he countered hotly. "I just want the two of you to accept your daughter's child. Is that too much to ask?"

Before the awkward moment escalated into an explosive confrontation, Bree took Charity from Eric's arms.

The baby was stirring now, stretching and rubbing her eyes, and making little whimpering sounds. Bree looked beseechingly at Mrs. Wingate. "The baby needs to eat. May I warm her bottle?"

Vivian looked momentarily flustered. "Oh, yes, of course. Come with me."

Bree followed her into the kitchen and waited, as the older woman placed the bottle in a pan of water on the stove. "I used to heat bottles like this for Eric and Marnie when they were babies. Women didn't breast-feed much in my day."

"Charity has taken to the bottle, although I've had to change her formula a few times. She's had some colic, but she's a good baby." Bree stroked Charity's cheek as the infant lay against her chest. "See? She senses her bottle is coming and stops crying."

Vivian tested the bottle and handed it to Bree. "My children were like that, too. Good babies. Always compliant and obedient. Never gave me a moment's trouble...until they were older, that is." She stirred something on the stove; it had a minty aroma. "Of course, Marnie was the difficult one. Not Eric. Eric was as good as gold. But Marnie—she pretended to be the obedient daughter, then went out and did exactly as she pleased. Lied. Thought we'd never find out about the baby. Where did it get her? She's dead and buried. And so are we."

Bree didn't let the remarks rankle. What good would it do to argue, to point out that the Wingates still had a great deal to live for? A loving son. An adorable granddaughter. But it was obvious Vivian Wingate saw the world only through her own jaundiced, judgmental eyes.

Bree sat down at the kitchen table and gave Charity

her bottle. The baby sucked hungrily, her round legs kicking the air with excitement.

"Excuse me," said Vivian coolly. "I'll finish setting the dining room table. We'll be eating in a few minutes."

"If you'd like some help, I'd be glad to—"

"Oh, no. You've got your hands full. I can manage."

The dinner hour went smoothly, considering its rocky beginning. Vivian served a sumptuous Christmas dinner—bib lettuce with a raspberry vinaigrette, roasted rack of lamb with mint sauce, small red potatoes and fresh string beans.

Charity lay quietly in her carrier, cooing, waving her arms and gazing up at the crystal chandelier, the gleaming china cabinet and the rose velvet chairs surrounding the massive table.

During dessert, as everyone feasted on Vivian's hot apple pie, Eric broached the subject Bree had been dreading all evening. Their engagement.

"Father, Mother, Brianna and I have an announcement to make."

The room was eerily still. Bree wanted to cry, *Stop, Eric! We can't carry on this charade, not in front of your parents!* But she held her tongue, as Eric gave her an indulgent smile and plunged in boldly. "The truth is, Brianna and I are engaged. We're going to be a family and make a home for Charity."

"Are you out of your mind, son?" countered his father.

"No, my mind is clear. Brianna and I are getting married."

Vivian clasped her cheek as if she'd been struck. "Oh, Eric, no!"

His father broke in sharply. "Why are you doing this,

Eric? Out of some twisted sense of responsibility to your dead sister? You have no obligation to raise her child. She made her choices. Let sleeping dogs lie!''

"No, Father." Eric's voice rose with an impassioned throb. "I admit that at first I wanted this for Marnie. But now it goes far beyond that. Bree and I are getting married because we love Charity and want to raise her as our own. We believe we can provide the best home for her. And we hope, we pray, you'll give us your blessing."

Vivian stared coldly at Bree. "Is this what it appears to be? A marriage of convenience? You say nothing of love."

Bree started to speak, but her mouth went dry. She stared in desperation at Eric.

"Bree and I care deeply for each other, Mother. And we're devoted to Charity. What more do we need to create a stable, nurturing home?"

Vivian turned a shrewd gaze on her son. "You're willing to settle for the arrangement your father and I have? A marriage in which we merely tolerate each other?" She cast a stony glance at her husband. "Don't deny it, Edward. You never would have married me if I hadn't been pregnant with Eric."

Edward Wingate slammed his linen napkin on his plate and shoved his chair back from the table. "And you'll never let me forget that, will you, Vivian!"

"Just as you never let me forget why you married me!"

Eric reached over and gripped his father's arm. "Mother! Father! Stop this incessant arguing and casting blame. What does it matter why you got married? You care about each other. I know it, whether you admit it or not."

His father sank back in his chair. "What good does it do to talk about it now?" He looked dubiously at Brianna. "We shouldn't be airing our dirty laundry in front of our guest."

Bree pretended to concentrate on a flaky morsel of crust.

"Brianna's not company," protested Eric. "She's going to be family. And I want us all to get along. I expect you to accept her as my wife and Charity as your granddaughter."

The Wingates remained silent. Brianna wanted nothing more than to jump up, grab Charity and run from their oppressive house. But she held her ground and finished her pie as if they had been discussing nothing more unsettling than the weather.

Finally, with a little huff, Edward Wingate boomed, "Welcome to the family, Miss Rowlands. If this is what you and Eric want, we'll do whatever we can to accommodate you."

"Thank you, Mr. Wingate." Bree said the words with quiet restraint, but she wanted to exclaim, *I don't know what I want. I'm afraid Eric and I are making the biggest mistake of our lives. But I don't know how to unravel this web we're spinning!*

"Thank you, Father," said Eric. "What about you, Mother?"

Vivian let her fork clatter on the china plate. "Well, I've had my say. If you two choose to get married, who am I to stop you? But if you're considering moving in here with that baby—"

"No, Mrs. Wingate," Bree said firmly. "We wouldn't do that." She wanted to add, *We wouldn't subject Charity to people who don't love her, even her own grandparents.* But she choked back the words. She and Eric faced enough obstacles without inciting the hostility of his parents.

"Actually, Brianna and I are shopping for a new home. We're hoping to put a down payment on a small house somewhere outside San Diego. Close enough for my drive to work, but far enough out in the country to give us a taste of nature and some open space."

"So you have it all planned," said his mother thickly. "Does this mean Brianna is giving up her counseling position?"

"I...I don't know," Bree admitted, with a quick glance at Eric. "I'm afraid we haven't discussed it yet."

"It'll take some time to work out all the details," said Eric, "but we're getting there."

Charity began fussing, so Brianna scooped her up and bounced her in her arms. "You haven't held your granddaughter yet, Mrs. Wingate. Would you like to hold her before we go?"

"Yes, Mother," said Eric forcefully. "I think it would be nice for you to hold Charity at least once. You might as well get acquainted. You're going to be seeing a lot of one another."

Vivian looked as if she were about to say no, then gave a little sigh and pushed her chair back from the table. "Do you have one of the baby's blankets I can put over my dress? I can't tolerate spit-up on an expensive outfit."

"Yes, this should do." Bree arranged one of Charity's blankets over Vivian's shoulder and then laid the baby in her lap. Vivian held her awkwardly for a moment, shifting her in her arms until Charity gazed up curiously into her grandmother's face and made a chortling sound.

"She likes you, Mother," said Eric. "Look at her smile."

Vivian's grimace melted into an embarrassed smile. "How could she like me? She doesn't even know me."

"Well, talk to her, Mother. One thing about Charity, she doesn't demand an intellectual conversation. She thrives on baby talk, laughter and funny sounds."

Vivian's smile widened as she stroked her granddaughter's plump cheek. "Well, you certainly are a good-looking child, Charity Wingate. Someday you'll give the boys a run for their money." Her smile waned. "And I hope you use better judgment about men than your mother used."

"Mother, please, don't hold Marnie's mistakes against an innocent child."

"I'll try not to. But don't expect me to become attached to this baby. I refuse to subject myself to more heartbreak."

"Don't you understand, Eric?" said his father in a weary voice. "Your mother and I are too old and too tired to invest our emotions in another child. We have enough to deal with, reconciling ourselves to Marnie's death."

Vivian handed the infant back to Brianna, then gazed frankly at Eric. "Your father's right. You may choose to sacrifice your life for your sister's child. But your father and I have nothing left to give. Don't expect us to be doting grandparents."

A frown shadowed Eric's eyes. "I don't expect anything, Mother. I never have. When I wanted love and acceptance as a child, I turned to Grandmother and Grandfather Wingate. I wouldn't be the man I am today if it weren't for them. But now you're the grandparents. All I ask is that you not close your heart entirely. You wouldn't believe how that sweet baby has eased my pain over losing Marnie. She could help you and Father heal, too.''

"Maybe you feel that way now," said Vivian solemnly. "But watch out. Someday you may find yourself resenting that baby for changing the whole course of your life. You think tying yourself down to a wife and child is the answer. But you might wake up someday and realize it's your worst nightmare.''

Eric was quick with a comeback. "And I just might discover it's my most glorious dream come true.''

The conversation ebbed after that. In her loftiest tone, Vivian suggested they all retire to the living room to open gifts. Gathering around the bay window, each one opened an impeccably wrapped package while the others watched in awkward silence. The Wingates were polite but less than enthusiastic over the presents Bree gave them—a pewter-framed portrait of Charity and a scrapbook of pictures and mementos of her first four months. Bree hoped the gifts would forge the tiniest chink in their hardened hearts for Charity. But if tonight was any indication of Christmases to come, they all faced a long, lonely, onerous road ahead.

Even the Wingates' silver tree with its gold bulbs and flickering lights seemed to strain to bestow holiday cheer. Brianna found herself missing the hectic revelry and excitement her family enjoyed when they tore open their gifts around a dazzling, bejeweled tree. Her home had always spilled over with love and warmth and joy. Compared to the Wingate household, the Rowlands family celebrated Christmas year round, always giving themselves freely, joyously to one another.

By contrast, Eric's parents clutched what little caring they possessed to their breasts, lest someone snatch it away. They had no idea how starved their children had always been for acceptance and affection. No wonder Eric seemed so determined to establish a loving family of his own. But could it be accomplished when that love hinged shakily on one small, helpless infant?

That was just one of the burdensome questions pressing on Brianna's mind that night, as Eric drove her home. She couldn't help noticing the tension in his jaw as he gripped the steering wheel. She knew he genuinely loved Charity, but was he marrying Bree just to defy his callous, unyielding parents?

"I guess that went as well as could be expected," Eric said dryly after a lengthy silence. "My parents weren't complete ogres. Close, but not complete."

"But what if they're right?" she ventured. "What if someday you do regret marrying me? What if we can't make it work? Do we want to risk being as miserable as they are?"

"They had to get married because my mother was pregnant."

"But you want us to get married for the sake of a child, too. Everything can't be just about Charity. What about us?"

He gave her a sidelong glance. "I don't see a problem, Bree. We have a good, stable relationship. I know you don't love me in a romantic way, but you do care. I see it in your eyes. I feel it when we're together."

But I do love you! she wanted to cry. *With all my heart and soul!* But the words wouldn't come. Her pride silenced her. To confess her love now would undermine the entire premise of their fragile alliance. Eric wouldn't, *couldn't* in good conscience marry her knowing he had her at such a psychological disadvantage. As long as neither of them was in love with the other, the relationship was fair, balanced, equal.

"We're good together, Bree," Eric was saying, oblivious of her inner turmoil. "All right, so it's not romantic love, but I hear that's highly overrated, anyway." He looked over at her and smiled that winsome smile of his. She loved the way the moonlight illuminated his handsome features. "I promise, Bree, I won't ask anything of you that you can't freely give. Maybe someday we'll grow to love each other in that special way. Until then, I'll appreciate what we do have—compassion, respect, companionship. Our faith. Mutual goals. And Charity."

Bree gazed out the windshield at the glittering red and green lights strung on houses and shops and across lanes and boulevards. In another hour it would be Christmas, a day of miracles. Could she ask for a miracle, too?

"When you talk, Eric, you make our future sound reasonable. But when I'm alone and think about what we're doing, it scares me. I feel this sense of panic. What am I getting into? Can I accept a loveless marriage without growing resentful?"

"It won't be without affection, Bree. It's not as if we have no feelings for each other. We care a great deal."

"But what about you? Won't you resent me someday, the way your parents resent each other? Do we want to risk destroying the genuine feelings we have for each other by committing to a future that's not honest? Marriage is hard enough for people in love. How can we make a go of it without love?"

Eric accelerated on the open freeway. "That's just it. People in love go into marriage with their heads in the clouds or their heads in the sand. They don't know what they're getting into. They're so blinded by love, they can't see the pitfalls. But it won't be like that for us. We'll go into marriage with our eyes wide open and our minds clear, so there won't be all the surprises and disappointments other newlyweds face. We'll be past all the sentimental, idealistic notions that sabotage other couples. Our relationship will be grounded in reality.''

As she stared out the window at the passing scenery, Bree heard every word Eric was saying. But somehow, in her heart of hearts, she had the disturbing sensation they were flying in the face of everything they held dear. Only time would tell whether they were about to make the biggest mistake of their lives.

Chapter Sixteen

❧

On the first Saturday of January, Eric phoned and invited Brianna to go house-hunting with him. "I think I've found us the perfect place. I'm just hoping you like it as much as I do. And I have another surprise. So what do you say? Are you free?"

"Of course. I can be ready in an hour."

"What about Charity? I hate to tire her out dragging her around to housing tracts."

"No problem. I'll see if Frannie can watch her."

In little more than an hour, Eric and Brianna were on their way to the Sunny Meadows housing development in southeast San Diego County, a community of custom homes nestled among towering oaks and stately eucalyptus trees. The moment Eric pulled into the model home's circular driveway, Bree knew she was looking at her dream house—a spacious two-story, Spanish-style hacienda with a charming courtyard and a sprawling yard of lush green grass.

"Oh, Eric, it's gorgeous. I love it already."

"I knew you would. I checked it out yesterday, and

I kept thinking, 'This is the house for Brianna.' Wait till you see inside."

In the formal marble foyer, a pretty young hostess handed them a brochure and offered to show them around. "Our homes offer three-car garages, full-yard fencing with automatic sprinklers, and hand-rubbed bronze exterior door hardware," she said in a light, musical voice as she led them through the high-ceilinged living room to the gourmet kitchen. "Notice the self-cleaning oven, trash compactor, natural oak cabinetry and roomy walk-in pantry." She obviously had her speech down pat. "Our energy-saving features include dual-glazed windows and set-back thermostats, and all bedrooms have smoke detectors. You may also upgrade your home with an intercom, central vacuum and water-filtration system."

"I'm already familiar with the house," Eric told the hostess, "so if you have other clients, we can find our way around."

The girl glanced from Eric to Brianna, then flashed a knowing smile. "Oh, okay. Sure. If you have any questions, just let me know."

Eric held Bree's elbow as they climbed the circular stairs to the master suite.

"Oh, Eric, this looks like a separate apartment." Her eyes traveled over the plush sitting room and luxurious master bath. "Look! There's even a balcony!"

"I knew you'd like it. We can put a little table and chairs on the balcony and have our morning coffee there. Or we can sip lemonades and watch the sunsets."

Bree drifted around the spacious bedroom as if moving in a dream. It *was* a dream—the tantalizing idea of living in this lovely house with Eric and Charity. Like a real family. She wandered into the master bath and ran her fingertips over the porcelain sink, ceramic countertops and bronze fixtures. "Look, Eric, a sunken tub with a Jacuzzi! And the walk-in closet is a room in itself!"

"Think it'll hold all our stuff?" he asked with a wink.

"If it doesn't, we'd better get rid of something."

She returned to the sleeping area and smoothed her palm over the plush comforter on the king-size bed. "Everything's so elegant. Imagine! A balcony, Jacuzzi and room-sized closet. I feel guilty at the thought of being so extravagant."

"Don't you dare feel guilty. I want you to have the kind of home you've always dreamed of." Eric drew her into his arms and kissed the top of her head. "Let me do this for you, okay, Bree? It'll make me happy to see you happy."

"I am happy," she murmured, feeling herself pulled into the smoky depths of his eyes. Just being in his arms was pure bliss.

He wound a ringlet of her hair around his finger. "In case you're wondering, Bree, this will be your room. I'll take one of the other bedrooms down the hall. I don't want you to feel I'm invading your space or intruding on your privacy."

A knot of disappointment tightened in her chest. For a moment she had almost convinced herself this would be a real marriage, in spite of what Eric had said. But, of course, he wouldn't want to share this room with her, this bed, when he had no intention of being a real husband.

"Oh, and Bree, I have a surprise for you." He led her over to the sitting area and joined her on the tufted floral love seat, then reached into his pocket and produced a small velvet box. "This is for you, Brianna. I should have done this when we first got engaged, but I wanted to wait until I found just the right one."

She gazed questioningly at him, then at the tiny black box. "Is this what I think it is?"

Eric opened the lid and revealed a perfect diamond mounted in a white-gold band. As Bree watched in mute astonishment, he removed the dazzling ring and slipped it on the third finger of her left hand.

"You...you didn't have to do this, Eric," she stammered.

"Of course, I did. We're engaged. You need a ring."

Another token of our sorry charade, she thought darkly.

"So it's official," he said, beaming. "And if you say the word, we'll make this house official, too."

"You want to buy it now? Today?"

"If this is the house you want, I'll put some money down to open escrow and the deal should close by our wedding next month. If it takes a few more weeks, that's okay. We'll be on our honeymoon, anyway."

"Our honeymoon?" Eric was full of marvelous surprises. She couldn't keep up with him. "What honeymoon?"

He took her hand and studied the ring on her finger. "After the wedding there's the honeymoon. You know that."

She gave him a slow, coquettish smile. "You never mentioned a honeymoon before."

"Because I wanted it to be a surprise. But if you like exotic locales with sandy beaches and moonlit sunsets, you're going to love this place."

She nestled against him. "It sounds wonderful! But

what about Charity? Who will take care of her while we're gone?''

Turning her face up to his, he broke into a spontaneous grin, his dark eyes crinkling at the corners. ''That's the beauty of it, Bree. We'll take her with us!''

Of course! Why hadn't she seen that blow coming. Naturally, Charity would go with them on their honeymoon. She was the only reason they were getting married in the first place!

''You don't mind, do you? I just assumed you wouldn't want to leave her for a week or two. She's still so young. And these days it's fairly easy to travel with a baby.''

''That's fine. You're right. I wouldn't want to leave her. Besides, who would we leave her with? My sisters both work.''

''And my parents...well, enough said.'' He stood up, pulled her to her feet and led her out of the master suite and down the hall. ''Speaking of Charity, you've got to see this next room! You're going to love it!''

She followed him into a warm, sunlit room with pink rosebud wallpaper and frilly lace curtains. ''Oh, Eric, it's breathtaking!'' It was an exquisite nursery with a gleaming white canopy crib, a Colonial dresser with brass knobs and a large changing table. A Cinderella lamp graced the dresser, and in a white antique rocker sat a family of old-fashioned teddy bears. ''You're right. This would be perfect for Charity.''

''I knew you'd like it. The furniture doesn't come with the house, but nothing says we can't duplicate what we've seen here.''

By the time they left the model home, Brianna's head was spinning. Eric had signed the papers and written a check for the deposit. They were in escrow for the house of her dreams!

For the next few days she could think of nothing but what it would be like when she and Eric and Charity moved into that magnificent house. Surely once they were all under one roof and living as a family, everything else would fall into place. Lots of couples fell in love *after* they were married. Didn't they?

On Wednesday evening, as Brianna was getting ready for prayer meeting, the telephone rang. She was running late. Her father and sister had already left. So she sounded impatient as she grabbed the receiver and barked hello.

"Miss Rowlands?" came a woman's tentative voice. "Brianna Rowlands?"

"Yes, this is she."

"This is Wanda Dillard. Sam Dillard's mother."

A stitch of alarm caught in Bree's stomach. "Yes, Mrs. Dillard?"

"I realize we're going to be facing one another in court next month, but I would like to speak to you, privately, if you're free sometime."

"I...I'm not sure our lawyers would think that's a good idea, Mrs. Dillard."

"I realize that, Miss Rowlands, but if there's any way for us to avoid going to court..."

"Are you saying Sam is willing to give up his parental rights, after all?"

"No, Miss Rowlands, I'm not saying that. But there are some things about Sam you may not be aware of. Would you let me come over and talk with you?"

"You mean now?"

"Yes, if I may. Please. This is very important to me...and my son."

- "All right. Come over. Do you need the address?"

"Isn't it the minister's house where Marnie stayed?"

"Yes. When she was expecting her baby."

"Then, I have it. I'll see you in about a half-hour."

While Bree waited, she wondered whether she should phone Eric and tell him what had just transpired. She had a feeling he would loudly protest a visit from the Dillards. But something deeper told her she had to do this, no matter what any lawyer said. No matter what Eric said.

Mrs. Dillard arrived exactly when she'd said she would. Brianna was already waiting by the foyer, pacing, her misgivings growing. As soon as she heard the bell, she swung open the door and welcomed the slender, pleasant-faced woman inside. Wanda Dillard was a delicate, diminutive version of Sam, with small, flashing dark eyes in a narrow face framed by a mop of tousled blond curls. She was wearing an oversize teal-blue sweatshirt, matching leggings and worn sneakers. Her features were a bit too sharp to be pretty and her tan skin had baked too often in the sun to be supple. It was hard to judge her age. She could have been as young as her late thirties or as old as fifty.

Brianna led her into the parlor and offered her a chair. "Would you like something to drink? Tea? Coffee?"

Wanda sat down in an overstuffed chair beside the weathered brick fireplace. She remained perched on the edge of the seat, as if she might decide to bolt at any moment. Bree took a chair opposite Wanda's, beside a small pedestal table. The two looked at each other as if each was waiting for the other to speak.

Finally Bree said, "You wanted to talk to me about Sam."

"Yeah." Wanda nervously massaged her long, tapered fingers. The nails were painted an odd color, not quite purple, not quite brown. "You got the wrong idea about Sam."

"The wrong idea?"

"You think he's the villain in this lousy situation. You think he deserted Marnie. You think he didn't want anything to do with her or the baby."

Bree struggled to keep her voice neutral. "To my knowledge that's exactly what happened. Sam never came to see Marnie. He wasn't there when his baby was born."

"True enough. But Sam loved Marnie. Problem is, she never told him about the baby until she was over six months pregnant."

"And when she told him, he was hardly supportive."

"Yeah, I know. Sam was shocked. He said the first thing that came to him. 'Get rid of it.' But he wasn't thinking. And by the time he could think straight, Marnie was gone."

"She didn't go far. He could have come after her."

"Yeah, sure. That's just what he tried to do. But her family told him she'd gone traipsing off to Europe to study. What was he supposed to think? He figured she got the abortion and ran off to who-knows-where because she didn't love him anymore. It wasn't until she and her big-time lawyer came to him with those legal papers to sign that he knew she hadn't had the abortion and run off to Europe. He was knocked for a loop to see her like that, big as a house, ready to deliver his child."

"He could have reconciled with her then. Before Charity was born. If he loved her, why didn't he?"

"Because she was coming on strong about him giving up his parental rights. He didn't know what to do.

He felt guilty and confused. He only signed the papers because that's what Marnie wanted. She seemed so desperate, he felt he had to give in. But it wasn't because he didn't want his child. He was afraid that if he refused to sign, he would upset Marnie in her precarious condition.''

Bree shook her head. *Lord, help me keep my emotions under control, please!* ''It's easy for you to say all of this now, Mrs. Dillard. But it doesn't change anything. Your son didn't come to see Charity until she was nearly three months old. Where was he all that time, if he cared so much about her?''

''He was grieving Marnie's death. Sure, he was reluctant to see the baby. He was afraid it would hurt too much. But once he saw Charity, it was love at first sight. Didn't he come see her every chance he got?''

''And now he wants to raise her? How's he going to do that, Mrs. Dillard? He's a college student living at home. He has—what? A part-time job? What can he give her?''

The muscles in Wanda's face tightened around her dark, bird-like eyes and chapped lips. She looked suddenly like a woman on a mission, like a woman who didn't know what it meant to give up.

''What can he give her? Sam can let her grow up with her real daddy and her real grandparents and a whole slew of other family members who want to get to know her. We're ready to make a home for her, Miss Rowlands. Sam and his stepdad have got the spare room all fixed up for her. You should see it. It's pretty as a picture, with a crib and blankets and toys.''

An ache was settling in Brianna's chest, heavy as a rock. ''I didn't realize…''

''And Sam's going to church now, because Marnie

told him she wanted her daughter raised in church. He's going to do everything right by his daughter, I can promise you that, Miss Rowlands. Please, please, give my boy a chance."

"That's not for me to decide, Mrs. Dillard."

"Sure it is. If you withdraw your petition for custody, the judge will give Charity to her daddy. Simple as that."

The weight of misery in Bree's chest was swelling to disquieting proportions. She couldn't catch her breath. "Please, Mrs. Dillard, don't ask me…"

"Who else can I ask, Miss Rowlands? You're a minister's daughter. That means you must pray sometimes."

"Yes. Every day."

"Then, pray about this. Ask God to show you what's right."

"I have. I do constantly. I want God's will in this, Mrs. Dillard. That's all I want."

Wanda pushed an unruly coppice of bleached curls back from her lined forehead. She leaned toward Brianna, and Bree caught the fragrance of vanilla. "Miss Rowlands, there's something else you don't know about my son."

"What is it?" Bree managed in a small, tight voice.

"Sam was only four years old when his dad walked out on me. On us. He never came back, never checked up on Sam, never wrote, never sent a birthday card or a Christmas present. It was like he just disappeared off the face of the earth."

"I'm sorry. I didn't know."

"Lucky for me, I met Sam's stepdad and he adopted Sam. Treats him like his own kin. But Sam never got over losing his real dad. He looks for him to this day, always thinking the jerk is going to waltz back into his life and start being a real father.'' Wanda's voice swelled, urgent and compelling. ''It's not going to happen, but Sam doesn't stop watching and hoping.''

Bree shifted uncomfortably in her chair. ''What does that have to do with Charity?''

''Everything. Sam doesn't want his daughter growing up thinking her real dad deserted her. He doesn't want her spending her life missing him and searching for him. It would break his heart to have her feeling she wasn't good enough for her daddy to love. Because he does. He adores her.''

Warm, salty tears gathered under Bree's lids. ''I'm sure he cares about her, Mrs. Dillard. But that doesn't qualify him to raise her. There's so much involved in raising a child today.''

''He's willing to learn. Give him a chance, Miss Rowlands. Like I said, pray about it. And God will show you what to do.''

Chapter Seventeen

❧

Andrew was excited. Now that his daughter Brianna had a diamond ring on her finger and money down on a house, it was time to let the world know her engagement was official. How better to announce it than to surprise her and her intended with a little celebration party in the backyard?

Thank goodness, his dear Juliana had agreed to help. In fact, she had taken the ball and run with it. Andrew himself had never been one to pull off successful parties. His idea of a gala event was to call a handful of friends at the last minute and say, "Hey, why don't you come over tonight and I'll throw some steaks on the grill? Yeah, pick up some chips and dip on your way over. And if you think of anyone else who should be here, give them a call. Tell them to bring some soda."

The moment Andrew had suggested the surprise party to Juliana, she had nixed the impromptu approach. "Andrew, darling, we must phone our guests at least a week in advance so they can write it on their calendar. And I'll plan the menu and provide the food. Otherwise, we will end up with six bags of chips and ten cartons of root beer, and little else!''

They planned the party for the second Friday of January, which gave Juliana a little over a week to invite the guests, order the food, and arrange for entertainment and decorations. Frannie and Cassie both quickly caught Juliana's festive spirit, and soon the whole affair was a major production. Antonio had even agreed to sing for the occasion. Since Eric and Brianna were planning just a small, intimate, "family only" wedding in February, this would be the only chance for many of their friends to celebrate with them and wish them well.

And now the grand moment had arrived. The party was about to begin. The guests had arrived and had been herded into the backyard, where sparkling grape juice was flowing from an actual fountain. (Where had Juliana found that?) And a vast, linen-draped table was resplendent with fancy canapés and hors d'oeuvres and colorful platters of fruit, breads, cheeses and sliced turkey and beef. Not to mention the fancy cakes, pastries and sweet chocolate truffles. A tempting, tasty feast fit for a king. Or for his daughter and her beloved.

Yes, Andrew mused as he gazed out the kitchen window at his guests milling about and sampling the culinary masterpieces, *my darling Jewel has done a magnificent job.*

She was a keeper, no doubt about that. And if he had his way, he would take advantage of this evening to announce his own engagement to the ravishing and irrepressible Juliana Pagliarulo. Of course, he would wait until the party was nearly over. He didn't want to steal any thunder from Eric and Brianna.

The only question now was, *Where were the guests of honor?*

Brianna had promised to be home by six. And Eric was supposed to be with her. They were going to spend a quiet evening taking care of Charity. Or so they thought.

While his guests enjoyed the backyard festivities, Andrew paced the floor inside, waiting for his daughter. His mind blazed with all sorts of alarming scenarios. What if they had changed their plans and not let Andrew know? What if at this very moment they were pigging out on double-cheese burritos at some fast-food drive-through? Or, God forbid, maybe they had been in an accident. *Take care of them, Lord, wherever they are. That's my precious girl out there.*

The kitchen door opened, letting in the sound of laughter and music from the backyard. Andrew whirled around. It was Juliana bustling in, her bright, rosy face animated with warmth and excitement, her lovely wreath of sable hair ruffled by the evening breeze. A red silk, pajama-style pantsuit nicely silhouetted her robust figure. Try as he might, he couldn't take his eyes off her.

"Andrew, where are they?" She shook his arm. "The guests are getting restless. They're ready to shout, 'Surprise'!"

He grimaced. "The surprise is…Brianna and Eric haven't shown up yet. I tried her cell phone—got a recorded message. Tried Eric's apartment—no answer. I even tried his parents' house, but they haven't seen him in weeks. I haven't the foggiest notion where they are."

A frown creased her smooth forehead. "If they don't come soon, we'll have to go on with the party without them."

"We just may do that." With a sly little chuckle,

Andrew grabbed Juliana's hand and pulled her into his arms. Heaven help him, how good she felt! Warm and soft, yet solid and reassuring. *A woman of substance.* Yes, that was Juliana. And she smelled so delectable. Of fresh roses and cinnamon and fresh baked bread.

Or maybe the bread smells were coming from the backyard. It didn't matter. He loved the smell of her and the feel of her and the taste of her. He kissed her earlobe and made a smacking sound. "Yes, indeed, you taste better than any of those goodies out there."

"Oh, Andrew, shame on you! What if someone is watching?"

"Who? There's no one else in here."

"They could see us through the windows."

"Then they'll get an eyeful, won't they."

She made an exaggerated pout with her full red lips. "And you…a respected minister, nibbling at a woman's ear."

He laughed and smoothed back her curls. "That woman is about to become my wife. I assume that should give me certain privileges."

She eyed him shrewdly. "Andrew, darling, you may nibble my ear anytime—except now when I am beside myself over this party. What are we going to do without our guests of honor?"

"I told you. We announce our engagement. And let everyone congratulate *us.*"

"You're serious, aren't you?"

"Got any better ideas?"

"No, but give Eric and Brianna a few more minutes. I will go out and have Antonio sing a song or two."

Moments after Juliana returned to the party, Andrew heard the door open in the foyer. He took long strides from the kitchen to the living room and reached the entryway just as Brianna came in and shut the door firmly behind her.

He looked around. "Bree...where's Eric?"

His daughter gazed at him as if to ask, *Why should you care?* He noticed now. Her eyes were red. She had been crying.

"Are you okay, honey?"

"I'm fine, Daddy. I...I just want to be alone for a while."

"Alone?" How could he tell her that three dozen party guests were waiting for her in the backyard? "I thought Eric was coming back with you this evening."

Brianna trudged into the living room and sank down on the sofa. "We had a little...disagreement. We need some space. I'm just really confused about a lot of things right now."

Andrew sat down beside her. "Anything I can help you with?"

She shook her head. "Oh, Daddy, it's too complicated."

"I'm willing to listen, sugarplum."

"Speaking of listening..." Bree crooked her head to one side. "I could swear I hear Antonio singing in the backyard."

Andrew felt the color rise in his cheeks. "Um, yes, I'm afraid so, Bree. That is Antonio. Singing. Sounds quite good, actually. Even without his sound system."

Brianna stared in bafflement at her father. "What on earth is he doing out there, Daddy? What's going on?"

Andrew scratched his head as if puzzling over a riddle. "Well, baby cakes, it's like this. We're sort of having a party."

Bree stiffened, her eyes darting to the draped windows. "Daddy, are you saying there are people out there?"

"Yes, that's about it."

Bree's hand flew to her mouth. "Lots of people?"

"Quite a few."

"How many?"

"Thirty...forty...give or take a few."

"Your Bible study group?"

Andrew reached over and clasped his daughter's hand. "No, honey, it's our friends and family. It was supposed to be a surprise party for you and Eric. To celebrate your engagement."

Bree's eyes widened in dismay. "Oh, Daddy, how could you!"

Andrew sat back and stared at his perplexing offspring. Was this the same girl who loved parties and looked for any excuse to have a family celebration? "Honey, I was just trying to do something nice for you and Eric. I know you don't have time to fuss with a big wedding because you've got to be married before your court date. So I figured, this way your friends could share your joy before the big event."

Bree began to weep.

Andrew put a hand out to comfort her, then withdrew it. "Honey, I never dreamed you'd be so upset. What's going on?"

"I...I can't talk about it! Just tell everybody to...to go home!" Sobbing, Bree scrambled off the sofa and bolted for the stairs. Andrew followed, several steps behind, and trailed her to her room, where she disappeared inside and slammed the door.

Andrew knocked soundly. "Talk to me, Bree. Please!"

Finally she opened the door and allowed him to enter.

Her usually expressive eyes looked desolate, ringed with shadows, as she slumped down on her bed and blew her nose into a tissue.

Andrew sat down beside her and gently pulled her against him. "Come on, kiddo, tell me what's wrong. How can a dad help if he doesn't have a clue?"

"It's awful, Daddy."

"Honey, let me be the judge of that."

"It hurts so much. My engagement to Eric…it's all a sham. He doesn't even love me. He's marrying me so he can get custody of Charity!"

"Whoa! You must be mistaken. If ever I saw two people who loved each other, it's you and Eric."

"Yes, I love him," Bree said between sobs. "But he doesn't even know I do. We agreed to have a marriage in name only so we could raise Charity together. He thinks I'm keeping my end of the bargain. But I couldn't stop loving him, Daddy. And now I feel so guilty and ashamed. I was wrong to agree to marry for any reason but love."

Andrew nodded. "You're right about that, honey. Marriage isn't just a contract between two people—it's a covenant with God. Not to be taken lightly."

"I know, Daddy. I just didn't want to lose Eric. I thought if I married him on his terms, he'd fall in love with me later."

"Have you tried telling him how you feel? Honestly?"

"Tell him I love him? I can't, Daddy. I couldn't bear to see the pity in his eyes. Right now we're on equal footing. We both know where we stand. But if he knew I was loping around like a lovesick calf, it would change the dynamics between us. He'd offer to marry me out of some warped sense of obligation."

"I don't think you're giving Eric the credit he deserves. Remember the verse in Scripture, 'You shall know the truth, and the truth shall set you free.' You won't know real freedom until you're honest with Eric."

"It doesn't matter anymore, Daddy. It's over between us."

"Over? Did you break things off tonight?"

"Not exactly." Bree drew a deep, shuddering breath. "I told him I'm thinking of giving Charity to Sam Dillard."

Andrew stared in astonishment at his baffling daughter. "Now you *do* have me speechless. You adore that little girl. You can't think of giving her up."

Bree gave in to another round of tears. "I don't want to, Daddy. I love her so much. But I keep feeling like God is telling me to let her go."

Andrew drummed his fingers lightly on Bree's arm. "Well, I admit it's hard to argue with the Almighty. But are you sure it's God telling you this and not just your own feelings of guilt?"

"I've been praying about it since Sam's mother came to see me last week. I can't marry Eric for the wrong reasons. And if we're not married, we can't..." She swallowed another sob. "We can't give Charity the kind of home she needs. Sam's mother says she and Sam and their family will give her a loving home. She begged me to let Sam be a father to his little girl."

Andrew pressed Brianna's head against his shoulder and massaged the back of her neck. He could feel her wet cheeks dampening his dress shirt. Neither spoke until Bree's sobs subsided and her breathing came naturally again.

For a long while they sat together in the darkened

bedroom, Andrew's little girl in his arms, as if she were still a child instead of a grown woman. Andrew could hear the lilting music and peals of laughter coming from the party outside. Juliana would be wondering where he had disappeared to now, but she'd just have to manage alone. She was good at working a party and keeping the fun and excitement high.

Finally Andrew tilted Brianna's chin up and looked her in the eye. "Sweetheart, I think it's time to dry your eyes and fix your face and come downstairs to the party."

She shook her head. "Daddy, I can't face people now."

"Well, I promise, honey, if you come join the party, Juliana and I will be making an announcement that will direct all the attention to us." When Bree looked puzzled, he winked. "Let's just say, one way or another, there's going to be a wedding. It's going to be big. And it's going to be soon!"

Chapter Eighteen

It was decided.

Charity was going home to Sam Dillard.

It would be the hardest thing Brianna had ever done.

She felt as if she were giving pieces of herself away, emptying out rooms of her heart of all that she held most dear. She felt stricken, numb, dazed. She was losing Eric. Losing Charity. Losing the hope of a home and family of her own. At least, this particular family that she yearned for so deeply.

But it was as if, having set her mind to the task, she could allow nothing to dissuade her. Eric tried. He came over every day for a week to persuade her not to return Charity to her father. He pleaded, cajoled and reasoned with her, until on Friday she almost relented. For a moment it seemed that Eric was promising her a real marriage. "Give us a chance, Brianna," he kept saying. "It's going to work. I know we can make it work."

But suddenly she realized he hadn't said the crucial words, after all. He had said, *We can make it work,* as if they were confronting a job or a task or a riddle. Not, *I love you…I can't live without you.*

Just, *We can make it work.*

As if they were talking about a piece of machinery Eric could fix, with levers and knobs and bolts and dials that could be adjusted or tightened or rearranged. He was so sure he could fix things, the way a tradesperson might come in and repair items in a house and make them workable again.

But matters of the heart weren't subject to tinkering and fine-tuning with wrenches and pliers and drills. Without love to give a marriage breath and life, it was doomed to molder under the weight of dormant, and eventually deadened emotions. Why couldn't Eric see that? Why couldn't he understand that without a deep, abiding love between them, there was no home, no family, no relationship? They simply would be going through the motions, like lifeless puppets on a string. She didn't want puppets and pretense. She wanted a real, live marriage.

But Eric was too blind to see it.

So she held her ground and, in spite of everything, insisted they give Charity to Sam Dillard.

"You'll regret this for the rest of your life," Eric told her hotly, the night before they were to deliver Charity to the Dillard family. They were at her home, alone in the parlor, with Charity upstairs asleep. The tension between them sizzled in the air like static.

"I regret it already," she retorted, going to the window and gazing out, "but it's the right thing to do."

He came over and put his hand out to touch her, but she drew back. He was wearing the blue rugby shirt she loved and trim stone-washed jeans. "But what about us…our engagement?"

"There is no engagement." She carefully removed the twinkling ring from her finger and handed it to him. She was doggedly going through the motions of a painful ceremony of estrangement. Disengaging herself bit by jagged bit from the man and child she loved. "I can't marry you, Eric. I don't know what I was thinking of. Marriage represents Christ's sacrificial love for His church. It's holy, sacred. We can't cheapen it with a loveless marriage. We were rushing ahead of God, doing what seemed most expedient, not waiting on His will."

"Why can't it be His will for us to raise Charity? We have plenty of love for her."

"Because God wants more for both of us than a marriage of convenience."

"That's not what it was going to be."

"Then, what? What, except a loveless marriage?"

"It was never that to me."

She shook her head wearily. "How else would you describe it?"

Eric ran his fingers distractedly through his wavy hair. "Who knows what love is, anyway? Whatever we have—whatever we *had*—it's better than most people experience in a lifetime."

"I'm sorry. It's not enough for me. We could talk until we're blue in the face and we're not going to resolve this."

Eric hit the windowsill with his palm, making her jump. "Then I guess you win, Bree. Neither of us is in a position to raise Charity alone, and you refuse to let us raise her together. So by default that leaves Sam Dillard."

"I'm sorry, Eric."

"Me, too. More than I can say." He gripped her

shoulder and turned her toward him. "But I promise you, Bree, I'm going to keep an eye on that boy, on the whole Dillard clan. And if they fail to give Charity the kind of life she deserves, I'll be taking them to court so fast their heads will spin."

Bree nodded. Eric's warm hand on her shoulder left her feeling weak inside. How she yearned to melt in his arms and tell him she'd marry him whether he loved her or not. *Dear Lord, help me to be strong, to do the right thing!* "I'll be staying in touch with the Dillards, too," she said in a small, resolute voice. "I made that a stipulation of our agreement. Sam knows he has to do right by Charity, or we'll both be on his case."

Eric let his hand drop from Bree's shoulder. "Then, I guess there's nothing more to say. Except…I want to go with you when you take Charity over to Sam's house."

"I was hoping you would. I don't want to go alone."

"If it's okay, I'll come early. I'd like to spend a little time with Charity…saying goodbye."

"Come whenever you want. I'll be here."

He flipped the diamond ring reproachfully in his palm and heaved a disgruntled sigh. "So it's not just Charity. It's over between us, too, whatever it was, this crazy thing we were trying to put together." He gave her a tight-lipped grimace, his shadowed eyes hard as rail spikes. "It's a real double whammy. I lose Charity. I lose you, too."

"I'm sorry." Bree turned her face away from Eric, lest he see her tears.

"You keep saying that. 'Sorry.' But 'sorry' doesn't cut it, does it. We had a plan—a good, workable plan—and you decide it doesn't suit your whims. I don't get it, Bree. In my work, when you have something on paper that works, you go with it. But with you, everything has to be about emotions. Well, feelings change like the wind. Feelings just get in the way. I offered you something stable and secure, and all you can do is talk about feelings. I hope you and your feelings will have a very good life together." He turned and started for the door.

Brianna swiveled around, brushing at a tear. "We can keep in touch, can't we, Eric?"

He paused and looked back at her. "Sure. On holidays maybe. On Charity's birthday. Drop me a postcard. Send me an e-mail. Whatever suits you. Good night, Brianna. See you tomorrow." He crossed the room with long strides and disappeared down the hall. Moments later she heard the front door slam.

After that, the only sounds echoing in the empty house were Brianna's convulsive sobs.

Eric arrived shortly before five the next evening, looking dapper but casual in a rust-colored polo shirt and tan slacks. Brianna greeted him in a black crewneck T-shirt and low-slung jeans. Informal dress for a momentous event. They would be saying goodbye to their darling Charity.

"Is she awake?" Eric asked as soon as he entered the foyer. His expression was anything but casual. The muscles in his face looked as if they had been tightened to the point of pain. His eyes smoldered with dark embers of anger and resentment.

"Yes, she's in her infant seat in the living room. She's been fed and changed and she's wearing her prettiest dress."

"You have all her things packed?"

"Yes, everything's upstairs. Two suitcases. If you don't mind bringing them down later." Brianna followed Eric into the living room. "The Dillards already have the big things...a crib and dresser and changing table. So I'll probably give the stuff I have to Goodwill."

"Yeah. Might as well." Eric went over to the infant seat on the coffee table, bent down and stroked the baby's rosy cheeks. "Hi, little sweetheart, my little baby doll girl," he said. "Aren't you the most beautiful girl in the world?"

Gently he lifted her out of her seat, her organza crinolines wafting around her in lacy clouds. "Little darling, you look just like a china doll. Prettiest little lady on earth. That's my girl. And, oh, you feel so good in my arms." Eric held her close against his chest and nuzzled her downy hair. Charity gazed around curiously, her blue eyes wide, a smile flickering on her round pink lips as she gnawed absently on her fist.

Brianna sat down on the sofa and watched, as Eric hummed a mindless tune and danced Charity around the room in an exaggerated pantomime of ballroom dancing. After a few minutes he sat down on the sofa beside Bree and jounced Charity on his lap. The baby gave a happy, high-pitched squeal.

"I don't know what I'm going to do without you, little girl," Eric went on softly. "You're the best thing that ever happened to me."

Hearing those words, Brianna turned her face away and choked back a sob. If only Eric had felt the same unconditional love for her that he felt for Charity. They could have made such a perfect family. But it wouldn't work to enter marriage by the back door—starting with a baby and hoping love came later. Bree wanted to hold out for the real thing—a man who loved her first and best of all...and on down the road would come the babies.

Eric stood up, cradling Charity in his arms. "I suppose it's time to go."

"Yes. I said we'd be there by seven."

Eric placed the baby in Bree's arms. "I'll let you say goodbye, while I get her car seat and belongings."

Charity made a soft cooing sound as Bree rocked her and kissed her silky hair. "You're my little angel baby," she crooned. "I'll always love you. No matter where you are, my prayers will follow you. They'll be winging around you like little doves. And I pray someday you'll go to Sunday school and learn about Jesus and how much He loves you. Your daddy promised to take you. And I'm going to make sure he keeps that promise."

Bree paused as she heard Eric clambering down the stairs with Charity's things. "Come on, Bree," he called briskly from the foyer. "We'd better get this show on the road."

For Brianna, the next hour took on a surrealistic aura, as if she were moving in the slippery, shadowy maze of a dream. This wasn't quite real. It couldn't be real—she and Eric driving in moody silence to the Dillard home, Brianna carrying a squealing Charity across the lawn to the modest, single-story tract house, the three of them solemnly greeting the Dillard family at their door—Sam, his mother Wanda and stepfather Pete.

As everyone drifted into the small living room with its homey Early American motif and Norman Rockwell prints, Bree wondered what she was doing here. What had possessed her to come to this place and relinquish this child she loved so desperately? *How could I have done this? How could I ever have thought this was the thing to do?* she cried inwardly as she forced a brittle smile in place and made idle chitchat.

"Miss Rowlands, we have been waiting all day for this moment!" With a wide, gratified smile, Wanda Dillard held out her arms for her chortling granddaughter. "Come here, my little chubby cheeks girl. Aren't you the cutest little thing? Yes, you are, you little sweet petunia!"

With aching heart, Brianna laid Charity in Wanda's waiting arms. Immediately, her own arms felt jarringly empty. The sensation was almost physical, as if something had been rent from her very sinew and bones. She wasn't prepared for the sudden wave of misgivings surging over her now. Everything within her told her to grab the baby and run out the door, and keep running. She closed her eyes and clenched her fists to quell the impulse.

Eric nudged her arm. "You okay, Bree?"

She drew in a deep breath, but the room was airless, oppressive, heavy with an odor of fried onions and cabbage.

Sam Dillard came ambling up to Bree in a too-large sweatshirt and baggy trousers, his curly blond hair as rumpled as his clothes. "Thanks for bringing my little girl home." Somehow he looked younger here in his own house, and a bit awkward and ill at ease. He leaned over his mother and tickled Charity under the chin. "Hey, pretty girl, we've been waiting for you. Wait till you see your new room."

Wanda turned to her son. "Do you want to hold her, honey?"

"Sure." Sam scooped Charity up and held her against his chest. She reached a pudgy hand out and clasped a lock of his hair. Sam laughed and allowed her to pull his head down to hers.

"Hey, sweetpea, you're not going to let me go, are you."

Charity gave a high-pitched squeal, half laugh, half chirp. Bree watched with a growing sense of desolation as Sam walked his tiny daughter around the room, pointing out articles of interest as if he were a tour guide.

"Look, Charity, here's the TV," he said in a light, singsong voice, so low Bree could hardly hear. "We'll watch Big Bird and the Muppets on *Sesame Street.* Won't that be fun? And here's the rocking chair where I'll rock you to sleep. Only you gotta ignore all the creaking sounds. And in the backyard there's a swing. It was mine, but now it's yours. I'll swing you so high you can touch the sky."

As she watched father and daughter interacting here in Charity's new home, Brianna felt suddenly out of place, as if she were an interloper trespassing on someone else's life. She had no business being here. This was Charity's world now—this quaint little house with her father and grandparents. Charity didn't need Bree anymore. She had her own kin. This was where she belonged.

"I...I forgot her diaper bag," Bree said over a rising swell of emotion. "It's in the car. It has everything Charity needs for the next few days—her bottles and cereal and formula. She's on a special formula that's easy to digest." The words spilled out in a nervous rush. "She has rice cereal every morning mixed with two ounces of her formula and a spoonful of strained bananas. The bananas make it sweet, otherwise she won't touch it. And be sure to give her her vitamins. Just fill the little dropper and squeeze the liquid gently down her throat. Otherwise, she'll choke. And her medical records are in her baby book in the smaller suitcase. The doctor's number and her vaccination record are—''

Wanda placed a reassuring hand on Brianna's wrist. ''I'm sure we'll find everything just fine, Miss Rowlands. If we have any questions, we'll be sure to phone you.''

Sam sauntered over with Charity. ''I guess you'll be wanting to say goodbye to her, Miss Rowlands.''

Sam's stepfather stepped forward and picked up the two suitcases sitting by Eric's feet. ''I'll just go ahead and take these to Charity's room, Mr. Wingate.''

Eric nodded, but Bree could see the misery in his face.

''Fine,'' he said briskly. ''I'll get the diaper bag and car seat.''

''We want you to see Charity's room before you go,'' said Wanda brightly. ''Sam put cute cartoon appliqués on the walls and matching curtains on the windows. And he bought her the biggest stuffed giraffe you ever did see. Goes clear to the ceiling. The whole room is pretty as can be for our little baby girl.''

Wanda Dillard's cheery voice faded to mere background noise, as Brianna gave Charity one last hug. She held her so close, Charity began to whimper. Weeping, too, Bree buried her face in Charity's fine curlicues. ''Good night, my precious baby,'' she whispered. ''I'll love you forever. You'll always be my little girl in my heart.''

Somehow, as if on cue, Charity began to howl in loud, labored caterwauls. Her round face turned red, her lower lip quivered and her entire body grew rigid. Before Bree knew what was happening, Wanda hastened over and swept Charity out of her arms.

''Maybe you'd better go now, Miss Rowlands. The

baby's getting overly stimulated.'' Wanda jostled the wailing infant up and down in a coaxing, agitated motion. ''There, there, sweetheart, you're going to be just fine. Don't cry, honey. Come on, sweetie. You're in your new home. Please don't cry.''

Bree reached instinctively for the sobbing child. ''I'll take her, Mrs. Dillard. I know how to calm her.''

Wanda sprang back, holding Charity out of Brianna's reach. ''Just go, please,'' she implored. ''She needs us to comfort her now. We can handle things just fine and dandy from here on out.''

Bree recoiled as if she'd been walloped in the stomach with a sack of cement. She could hardly catch her breath as she stammered, ''I-if you need me, you know where to reach me.''

Summoning strength she didn't know she had— God's strength—Brianna endured the next few moments without collapsing. She and Eric each gave the baby a brief hug, then caught their last glimpse of Charity, as Sam whisked her away to her new nursery. After strained farewells to the Dillards, they made their way outside to the small lattice-trimmed porch.

But even after the door had shut soundly behind them, Bree could hear Charity's muffled cries inside. *She wants me,* Bree thought dolefully. *I'm the only mother she's ever known. She'll think I deserted her, stopped loving her. I'm the one she wants rocking her to sleep tonight. It's my arms she wants around her. Only my voice and my touch will soothe her.*

As Eric drove Brianna home in stony silence, she agonized, *Oh, God, what have I done? I've given up the best thing in my life because I was too proud to accept marriage on Eric's terms!*

Chapter Nineteen

It was like a death.

For Brianna, it was as if Charity had ceased to exist. For the first few days after delivering the baby to the Dillards, Bree waited for a phone call, expecting Sam and his mother to need her help, her advice, the benefit of her experience with Charity.

But no calls came.

Time and again she picked up the phone and started to dial Sam's number. But each time, she hung up the receiver, afraid that her interest would be perceived as interference. If she phoned, she might hear herself announcing that she wanted Charity back, that she couldn't live without her, after all. She couldn't trust herself to phone them, couldn't be sure she wouldn't dissolve into tears and act like a crazy woman. She had to keep reminding herself that Charity was Sam's responsibility now. She had let go physically; now she had to let go emotionally.

For the most part, she remained out of touch with Eric, as well. At first, he called her two or three times to tell her he had phoned Wanda Dillard and checked on Charity. "She's doing okay…some eating problems, but it's probably because she's in a new environment," he reported during one of his calls.

After a while Bree asked Eric not to call her unless there was a problem with Charity. "Keep tabs on her, Eric," she admonished. "Every day, if you want. But don't tell me every time you call the Dillards. I can't bear to hear about her."

"Then, I guess there's no reason for me to call you at all, Bree, is there," he said tonelessly.

"No, I suppose not." How could she tell him that it wrenched her heart as much to hear his voice as it did to hear news of Charity? She had made the supreme sacrifice, giving up the two people who meant the most to her, and now she was having a hard time remembering just why she had placed herself in this unbearable situation. It had something to do with not living a lie and not settling for second best, but, at the moment, lofty principles and platitudes offered little warmth or comfort.

Two days after handing Charity over to the Dillards, Brianna returned to her position at the family counseling center. For the next few weeks she threw herself into her work, pouring her energy and concern into her clients and their problems. When she returned home each night, she was too weary to do anything but collapse into bed. And that's the way she wanted it, so she wouldn't have to think about Eric and Charity and feel the deep abscess of pain festering in her heart.

"Why are you doing this to yourself?" her father asked her late one evening, when she dragged herself into the house after a twelve-hour day. He was in his velour robe and slippers, and had his favorite study Bible tucked under his arm.

"Why am I doing what, Daddy?" she asked evasively.

"This—" Her father smoothed back her mussed hair. "You're exhausting yourself. Killing yourself with work. You're going to make yourself sick, sweetheart."

"I'm fine, Daddy."

"You don't look it, honey. You know, you can't fool your old man. I know you like a book. Frannie has noticed, too. So has Juliana. We're all worried about you, sweetheart."

"There's nothing to worry about. It's just a period of adjustment. You know, get back into the grind at work and all."

Her father led her over to the sofa and pulled her down beside him. His arm went around her, and he nudged her head onto his shoulder. "Remember when you were little? When you fell off your bike and got hurt or someone at school teased you and hurt your feelings, you'd come home looking like a little Sad Sack."

"You always said I made the saddest faces in the world."

He chuckled. "It's the way your lower lip would drag on the pavement. No one could mimic that expression. I'd try to get you to tell me what was wrong, and you'd sit there in stony silence while big tears glazed your eyes and your lower lip trembled. And when you couldn't hold it back any longer, you'd let the tears flow, and it would all spill out—whatever had hurt you. We'd cry and pray together, and afterward we'd both feel better. Remember? We'd start laughing and end up in the kitchen popping corn or raiding the fridge. And whatever had hurt you would seem small and insignificant after that.''

Bree stiffened. "I'm not a little girl anymore, Daddy. You can't just kiss this away like a hurt elbow or a skinned knee. Nobody can make these hurts go away."

Her father drummed his fingers on the worn Bible on his knee. "I can't take away your pain, but we both know who can."

Brianna sighed. As much as she loved her father, she wasn't in the mood for a sermon tonight. "I know, Daddy. Don't say it."

"I know you know, sweetheart. But knowing something and experiencing it are two different things. I know God's Word because I preach it several times a week. But I don't experience His peace and joy and comfort unless I stay in touch with His Spirit, keep up my end of the communication. Otherwise, I'm like a lamp that's plugged in but not turned on. I may be connected, but I won't experience His light unless I'm turned on to Him."

"Why are you telling me this, Daddy? I know it already."

"But you're not experiencing that connection with Him right now. I can see it in your glum expression. You feel like the Lord has deserted you."

Bree could never resist her father's not-so-subtle fireside chats, one hand holding his Bible, the other offering a comforting hug. Suddenly she felt like that wounded little girl who yearned for nothing more than her father's healing touch. Only, now it was her Heavenly Father's touch she needed most.

"I'm trying to stay in touch with Him, Daddy, but sometimes it's so hard."

He squeezed her arm. "I know it is, honey. You

know how I struggled with God when your mother died. It took a long time of pouring out all my anger and bitterness and resentment, before I started feeling that closeness with Him again. But God has big shoulders. He can take it. Tell him honestly what you're feeling. You can't begin to heal until you can be honest with Him. Until you can sit in His presence and be yourself with all your questions and heartaches and misgivings."

Bree nuzzled her wet cheek against her father's broad chest. "Sometimes I don't even feel like God cares about me anymore, Daddy. He just seems so distant, so remote, so unconcerned."

"Baby, that's so far from the truth. Jesus said even the hairs of our head are numbered. You know how often that number changes, especially for you gals who brush a hundred strokes a night!" Her father expelled a hearty laugh that rumbled in his chest. "That verse is saying God cares about the most intimate details of our lives. Think of Him keeping constant track of the hairs on our head. You can't ask for anyone to be more in your face than that."

Brianna joined in her father's laughter. "Oh, Daddy, you have such a droll way of putting things."

"Tell you what. Let's go to the kitchen and pop us up a bag of microwave popcorn. The kind with the most butter. What do you say?"

She sat forward and gave him her most impish smile. "I say, it's time to bring out the big bibs because we're going to be swimming in butter."

By the time Brianna headed for her room that evening, she felt better than she had in weeks. Hopeful again. Positive. Confident. Her Heavenly Father still held her in the palm of His hand. He was still in control.

Before she climbed into bed, she curled up in the

comfortable overstuffed chair by the window and gazed out at the twinkling mid-March sky. It was time to connect with her Savior beyond her usual dutiful prayers. "Jesus," she whispered into the darkness, "I've been so consumed with Charity and Eric, I've lost my closeness with You. I didn't even realize how far away I'd drifted. I know You wanted me to let them go, and I'm trying, but I can't seem to get past the pain."

She was silent a while, gazing out at the deep indigo heavens, listening to the gentle quiet of stars and ticking clocks and rustling breezes, letting her muscles unwind as she received the Holy Spirit's healing balm.

A line from an old hymn played in her mind. "You take the whole world but give me Jesus." She knew, yes, had lived, the truth of that stanza, but all too often she let its message slip away. Too often she was distracted by her own compulsive plans and desires. Yet the truth remained. Give everything to Jesus. He is all you need.

She believed it, but hadn't been living as if she did. Could she live it now, when she had lost the two most important people in her life? Could she still find all she needed in Christ? *"Help me, Lord,"* she prayed urgently. *"I can't get through this ordeal in my own strength. I feel so weak and helpless. Help me to find everything I need in You. In the midst of my anguish, Father, please be my deepest joy."*

Somewhere at the back of her mind, the unsettling thought came to her, *Hold on tight to your Savior, Brianna, because you haven't learned the meaning of trouble yet. If you think the worst is over, wait until you're caught in the next tidal wave.*

Chapter Twenty

The phone call came in the dead of night.

Brianna had stumbled out of bed and put the receiver to her ear before the gauzy tendrils of sleep had cleared. With a dry, cottony mouth she croaked, "Hello?"

The voice on the other end sounded frantic. "Miss Rowlands...Brianna, this is Wanda Dillard."

For a moment Bree couldn't make the connection. Who would be calling at this hour? A wrong number? But as awareness took root, she felt a chill of comprehension. "Wanda? What's wrong?"

"It's the baby, Miss Rowlands."

Brianna's heart began hammering. "Is she okay?"

"No, she's sick. Awfully sick. I don't think she's going to make it, Miss Rowlands."

Every sinew in Bree's body tensed. "What's wrong with her?"

"I don't know. She's weak and feverish and throwing up. She just keeps getting sicker and sicker."

"Why didn't you call me?"

"We didn't want you thinking we couldn't take good care of her. I swear we did everything we could."

Bree grabbed her shirt and jeans. "I'm coming over."

"No! We're not at the house."

"Then, where?"

"We're at Children's Hospital on Health Center Drive."

Bree's heart stopped. "Charity's in the hospital?"

Wanda's voice took on a pitiful mewling tone. "She couldn't breathe. The poor little thing was turning blue. Choking, gasping for air. I thought she'd die before we got her here."

"No, God, no!" The words were raw, half prayer, half deep, visceral lament. Bree reached for her sneakers. She had kicked one under the bed and couldn't reach it. Her hands were trembling. "I'll be there as soon as I can."

"It's right by Sharp Memorial Hospital, south of where the 163 and 805 intersect."

"I'll find it."

"Miss Rowlands, would you call Mr. Wingate and tell him?"

"Yes. He'll want to be there." Brianna turned on the bedside lamp and sank down weakly on her bed. "Wanda, wait, don't hang up yet." Her mind was spinning like a child's top. Only faster, out of control. She couldn't think straight. What else did she need to know? Had to stay in touch with Wanda. She grabbed her purse off the dresser and fished inside for her cell phone. Yes, she'd need it. She gave Wanda the number and pleaded, "Call me if there's any news. Anything whatsoever."

"I will, Miss Rowlands. Sam's here with his little

girl. They're running tests, but we'll be by her side all we can."

"Tell her I love her." The words broke from Brianna's lips in a shuddering sob. "Tell her... Mommy's coming."

Brianna pressed the button for a dial tone and dialed Eric's number with cold, clumsy fingers. She was operating on reflex now, her senses numb, her breathing shallow and urgent. But her perceptions were heightened to the point of pain. She was moving and reacting in crisis mode.

Answer, Eric! Why aren't you answering? As she waited for him to pick up, she fetched clean socks and lingerie from her drawer and made sure her wallet was in her handbag.

Finally, Eric came on the line. She related the news with as much composure as she could muster, but she knew Eric heard the fear and desperation in her voice.

"Charity's ill? For Pete's sake, what happened?"

"I don't know, Eric. But we've got to get to the hospital."

"I'm on my way. Get ready. I'll swing by and pick you up."

"Hurry!" She collapsed back on the bed, feeling faint. Thank God, Eric was driving. He would be there for her. Whatever happened, she wouldn't have to face it alone!

He arrived in fifteen minutes. Must have broken all speed records to get there. But it was the middle of the night and traffic was light. Wordlessly she piled into his car and snapped on her seat belt. She stared straight ahead, as he pulled into the street and accelerated.

It had been weeks since she had seen him. Surely there was much to say, but at the moment her mind was as blank as her body was numb. Only one thought echoed in her mind over and over, like a mournful refrain; I never should have let Charity go. She'd be okay if I hadn't let her go!

The drive to Children's Hospital took nearly a half-hour. As they sped along the freeway, Eric was as tense and closemouthed as she. But what was there to say? They had lost their little girl once. Now they might lose her again. But that first loss was nothing compared to this new threat.

Eric dropped Brianna off at the entrance, while he went to park the car. She entered the sprawling lobby and hastened to the information desk, where a pleasant-faced lady gave her directions. She took the elevator upstairs, angled down several corridors and finally found the Dillards in a small waiting room.

Sam saw her first and came striding over, his narrow face blanched, his sandy, ragtag hair more wild than usual.

Brianna stared up at him. "How's Charity?"

He raked his fingers through his mop of curls. "I don't know, Miss Rowlands." His angular features had a fragile, crimped quality, his eyes squinty and red-rimmed, his lips drawn tight over his teeth. A bluish pulse throbbed in his temple. "I swear it's not my fault. I didn't do anything wrong."

Bree gripped his arm with strength that startled her. "Tell me what happened. What's wrong with her?"

Wanda Dillard joined her son and twined her arm in his. "We don't know what's wrong. The doctors are examining Charity now."

Eric came striding up, agitated, breathless. He slipped his arm around Bree's shoulder, as if the four were drawing up sides. "Where's Charity? What are they doing for her?"

Pete Dillard, a rangy, rumpled man with a lined face and thinning hair, left his vinyl chair and ambled over. He seemed shorter, heavier than Bree remembered. "Might as well sit down. The doctors said it might be a while before we hear anything."

They all sat down in the molded vinyl chairs, Bree and Eric facing the Dillards. "Tell us everything," said Eric, sitting forward, cracking his knuckles.

"Charity's been sick a lot," said Sam, his blue eyes narrowing, his lower lip twitching. "She wouldn't eat good. She was fussy. Cried a lot. We changed her formula. Didn't help."

"We figured maybe she had allergies," said Wanda, "so I took her to the doctor, and he said some babies are naturally more fretful and colicky than others."

"Charity was finicky sometimes," conceded Bree. "I changed her formula, too, but she wasn't fretful like you're describing."

"When did she get sick?" asked Eric urgently.

"This morning," said Wanda. "She was throwing up a lot, but I figured maybe she had the flu. She was listless and had a little fever and couldn't keep anything down. Finally, we got her to bed and we thought she was okay."

"But when I checked on her," said Sam, "she was choking and turning blue. Scared me out of my wits. Thought she was dying."

A knot of revulsion tightened in Bree's stomach. For a moment she was sure she was going to be sick. She turned her gaze to the nurses' station. "Where's the doctor? He must know something by now."

"I'll check," said Eric. He crossed the room and

spoke to the woman at the desk. She said something, gesturing toward a closed door, and after a moment Eric came striding back, a scowl on his face. "They won't tell you anything. She says we have to wait for the doctor."

They waited for another half-hour before a stout, balding man in a white lab coat and surgical trousers emerged. He was a swarthy man with a black mustache and a thick, fleshy neck that enveloped his round double chin. He approached with a rolling gait and held out a beefy hand. "Hello. I'm Dr. Moreno." He gazed over wire-rimmed spectacles at Brianna. "Are you the mother?"

"No." Eric spoke up. "Charity's mother is dead." In his "attorney" voice he introduced everyone and offered an abbreviated explanation of the situation.

"Let's sit down," said Dr. Moreno, sounding fatherly. When they had taken their seats, he pulled a chair over and sat down in the middle. Something about his portly frame, submerged chin and ball-bearing eyes couched in pouches of skin reminded Bree of a sage, ponderous walrus.

Bree uttered the question that was burning on her lips. "Is Charity going to be okay?"

Dr. Moreno made a little noise low in his throat. "I'm not going to sugarcoat this, Miss Rowlands. We have a very ill baby on our hands."

"Tell us everything," said Eric. "We want to know exactly what we're up against."

"All right. I've examined the child, and we've run a number of tests. Her respirations are rapid and unstable, and she appears severely dehydrated..."

"Because she couldn't keep anything down," said Wanda.

"And we suspect she's anemic. She appears to have recently lost a significant amount of weight."

"Yeah, she's skin and bones," said Sam. "She hasn't been eating right for days. We tried everything to make her eat, but she wouldn't. She'd spit up a lot and then choke and gag."

"She's experiencing projectile vomiting, which suggests she might have swallowed a foreign body," said Dr. Moreno. "It could cause a stomach upset, even a herniation of her intestinal wall."

"Is that serious?" asked Bree.

"Depends. Her belly was tender when I pressed it. And my stethoscope detected abnormal bowel tones. If she were a newborn, I'd suspect pyloric stenosis."

"What's that?" asked Sam, sounding appalled.

"An opening in the stomach. A birth defect. But as I understand it, the child has been relatively normal for most of her seven months."

"She was fussy sometimes," said Bree. "I had to change her to a soybean-based formula when she was a month old or so."

"But you observed none of her present symptoms?"

"None whatsoever." Bree drew in a sharp breath. "Dr. Moreno, when can we see her?"

"We're sending her to radiology now. We'll do a battery of X-rays and an MRI to rule out any problems with her heart."

"Please, can't I see her just for a minute," pressed Bree.

Dr. Moreno heaved himself out of his chair. "All right. One minute. No more. And go in quietly, two at a time."

"You go ahead," Sam told Eric. "You haven't seen her yet."

Bree's heart hammered in her chest as she and Eric entered the sterile cubicle and saw an unadorned metal crib surrounded by an array of formidable equipment. Bree stole over to the bed and gazed down in dismay at the child she loved so dearly. The frail infant that lay sprawled like a limp rag doll couldn't possibly be her darling Charity. This child had glazed eyes and a gray pallor, and her little ribs showed as she panted for every breath. A maze of tubes traveled in and out of her gaunt body as if she were a curious little marionette on strings.

Brianna's knees buckled, and she clutched Eric's arm in desperation. "Oh, my baby. My poor baby!"

Eric gathered Bree against him, his arm circling her waist. "She's going to be okay, hon. We've got to believe that."

"But she isn't okay! She...she could be dying!"

Eric tightened his grip. "Be strong. Be strong for her."

"I'm trying." She felt the weight of his sturdy chest against her shoulder, solid, warm, reassuring. "But how can I be strong when we're losing our little girl again?" She stared up at him with wet, desolate eyes. "I thought the worst had happened when we gave her up. But this...oh, Eric, if she dies I want to die, too!"

Eric nuzzled the top of her head, his lips moving over her tawny locks. He began to speak, and she thought he was addressing her. Then she realized he was praying, his voice low and fervent. *"Our Father-God, please heal this child we love so much. Help the doctors discover what's making her ill. Bring her back to us, please!"*

A nurse peeked inside. "I'm sorry, you'll have to go. The orderlies are here to take the baby to radiology."

Brianna touched Charity's feverish cheek and

brushed back her corn-silk curls. "We'll be praying for you, sweet Charity. I'll always love you, angel baby."

She and Eric returned to the waiting room, where Sam was pacing the floor, Wanda was thumbing listlessly through a magazine, and Pete was dozing in his chair. Eric went to the coffee machine on the opposite wall and came back with two cups of coffee. He offered them to Sam and Wanda, but they declined, so he sat down beside Bree and handed her one.

"Careful, it's hot."

"I'm not sure I can drink it."

"You'd better. It's going to be a long night."

It turned out Eric was right. It was nearly two hours before Dr. Moreno reappeared. He was carrying a medical chart, and the pouches under his eyes seemed more pronounced. "We have some results from radiology. Charity's heart is fine, but we've found some shadows that suggest her stomach is out of position."

Bree sat up, her skin bristling. "What does that mean?"

"We're going to have to operate."

"When?" asked Eric.

"The sooner the better. We're prepping her now."

Sam pushed a tangle of wayward curls back from his forehead. "She'll be okay, won't she?"

"We have every expectation that she will be."

"Then, she'll be back to normal, like she was?" pressed Sam. "She's not going to be a sickly little kid all her life, is she?"

"I can't answer that, son. Depending on what we find, she may need a feeding tube in her side for an indeterminate time. I'll have a better idea when we come out of surgery."

Dr. Moreno excused himself then, leaving everyone

with scores of unanswered questions. "There's so much more I wanted to know," said Bree, "but I didn't even know what to ask."

Sam got up and started pacing again. "Man, a feeding tube. They're gonna make my baby some kind of freak!"

"They're going to do whatever needs to be done," Wanda said to him. "We're just going to have to deal with it the best we can."

Eric reached for Brianna's hand. "Looks like we've got a few more hours to wait. It could be morning before we have any news." He lifted her chin. "You look exhausted. Why don't you try to get some sleep?"

She grimaced. "Sleep. How? In these chairs?"

He took her hand and pulled her to her feet. "Come on, there's a waiting room beyond this one, and I noticed a sofa. The comfy overstuffed kind." He turned to Wanda. "If the doctor comes, we'll be in the next room. I want Bree to get some rest."

Wanda nodded. "We'll call you."

The adjacent waiting room was empty, the lights lowered. It was smaller and more homey than the other room, the sort of private spot where doctors broke bad news to patients and their families. Eric sat at one end of the sofa and pulled Brianna down beside him.

"Get comfortable, Bree. Stretch your legs out and lie back. That's a girl."

Brianna was too tired to argue. Besides, there was something immensely consoling about the way Eric was taking charge, not to mention the sweet comfort of lying in his arms. If she weren't so worried about Charity, she could lie here forever in the tender embrace of the man she loved.

"One thing about it being the middle of the night,

we have the place to ourselves." His fingertips massaged her forehead. "Feel better?"

"Much." She gazed up at his handsome, careworn face. He was such a vigorous, valiant man, and yet in the golden lamplight he looked like a guileless little boy. "Are you going to sleep?" she asked.

"No. I'm going to pray for our little girl."

"Me, too." But in the midst of her prayers, Brianna drifted into slumber, her prayers meshing with her dreams. And in her dreams she saw the three of them—Eric and Charity and herself—walking hand in hand on a sparkling, sun-washed beach, laughing and singing and watching the gulls soar overhead in a cloudless sky. Strange, because Charity wasn't a baby anymore; she was a healthy, beautiful little girl. The scene was so real that when Bree woke, she was certain the three of them were still on that pristine beach, destined to be together forever.

Then she realized she was still in Eric's arms, and for a moment the realization warmed her...until she remembered where they were and what they were waiting for.

She stirred and gazed up at him. "Any news?"

"No, nothing yet."

"How long has it been?"

"Two hours."

"Shouldn't we have heard something by now?"

"Soon, I hope."

"The longer it takes, the more serious it could be."

"Not necessarily."

"You're just saying that to make me feel better."

"No, I mean it—"

As if on impulse, he lowered his head to hers and brushed a kiss on her forehead. Was she still dreaming?

No, this was real. His eyes glinted like twinkling slivers of moonlight. In his warm, enveloping arms she had never felt more cherished, more protected.

"God has given me a peace about everything, Bree," he said in that deep, soothing, take-charge voice of his. "We're going to be okay. All of us. We just have to trust Him."

She nestled her head against his chest. "I do. I want to."

His arms tightened around her. "I've missed you, Brianna."

"I've missed you, too." If he only knew how much!

"No, I mean I've *really* missed you. More than I ever imagined possible."

"Me, too," she confessed. Where was this going? What was he trying to say?

"I was watching you sleep," he went on, his tone hushed, his gaze hypnotic. "You looked like a little girl. So innocent and vulnerable. And I kept thinking, I want to take care of you. I want to be with you always. I don't want to let you go."

Bree's heart quickened. Was it possible? Did he feel half of the love that she was feeling? She sat up, still in the crook of his arm, and looked at him, their faces so close she could feel the warmth of his breath. "What are you saying, Eric?"

"I'm not sure, Bree. Except, we dropped the ball somewhere in this relationship thing. We were so close. We almost got it right, you know?"

"Yes. Almost."

He drummed his fingers on her arm in an unwitting rhythm. "You broke our engagement because you didn't want a loveless marriage."

She nodded. "I may be old-fashioned, Eric, but I have to hold out for true love."

"I understand that. But I've got another proposition, if you're willing to listen."

Her heart sank. Not more cerebral wrangling and negotiating! She couldn't contend with his logical extrapolations at a time like this. "I'm sorry, Eric. I don't think I can handle any mental gymnastics right now."

"I'm not going to lay any double-talk on you, Bree. My offer is simple. Would you be willing to enter a marriage if one party were in love?"

She stared at him in alarm. Had he discovered how much she adored him and decided that was enough to base a marriage on? It might be enough for him, but it surely wasn't enough for her. She wanted a man who... who worshiped the ground she walked on. Okay, maybe that was overkill, but she refused to settle for anything less than pure romantic love. But how could she begin to convince him?

"Eric," she said tonelessly, "please, I don't want to discuss this anymore."

He rushed on with an urgency and fervor she'd never heard before. "I've got to get this out, Bree. Let me have my say, and then I'll never speak of it again. I know you don't love me, not the way a woman should love her husband. But it doesn't matter to me."

She listened, framing arguments in her mind to toss back at him, until he said the words that she had only imagined hearing in her most fanciful dreams.

"It doesn't matter whether you love me, Brianna, because...because I have enough love for both of us!"

Chapter Twenty-One

Brianna stared in stunned amazement at Eric, as if he had suddenly sprouted extra ears or had just sung an aria from *Madam Butterfly*. Had she heard him right, or was her mind playing cruel tricks on her? Had he just said he had enough love for both of them? Did that mean…?

He still held her in the circle of his arms, his eyes trying to read hers. "Do you understand what I'm saying, Bree?"

She shook her head. She felt like a schoolgirl trying very hard to master her lesson…and failing miserably. "Say what you mean, Eric. Please. I'm afraid to presume anything."

He fingered her flyaway curls, one by one, his dark, beguiling eyes hypnotizing her. "I love you, Bree. I think I've loved you from the beginning, but I didn't realize what it was until I lost you. These past weeks without you have been pure torture. I kept trying to convince myself I didn't need you, didn't want you, didn't love you. I never pleaded a case so diligently...nor lost so utterly.''

"Oh, Eric..."

''I know you're not in love with me, Bree, but if you would give me a chance, I swear I—''

She stifled an amused titter. "Eric, don't you know?''

"Know what?''

She cupped his fine, sculpted jaw in her palms. "I love you, too. I've loved you since Marnie first showed me your picture. And I'll love you for the rest of my life.''

"You love me?''

"I adore you.''

As the light of comprehension illuminated his face, he broke into a magnificent, mischievous grin. "Well, then, my darling, what's all this talk about a loveless marriage if we're both head over heels?''

She covered her mouth but couldn't hold back a bemused chortle. "Oh, Eric, this changes everything, doesn't it.''

He tilted her face up to his and kissed her soundly. "I've wanted to do that for so long. I've wanted the right to do it, the right to kiss you and hold you and cherish you forever. I know this isn't the time or place, but I've waited too long already. Bree, will you accept my engagement ring...again?''

Her expression clouded. "I want to, Eric, but I can't make a commitment like that tonight. Not when we don't know what's going to happen to our darling Charity.''

Eric's smile vanished. He nodded, his brow furrowing. "For a moment I almost convinced myself we weren't sitting here waiting for her to come out of surgery.''

"She has to be all right, Eric. I couldn't bear to have anything happen to her. But even if we marry, we won't have her with us...our little girl."

"No, we won't." Eric clasped her hand, intertwining his fingers with hers. His eyes held a solemn intensity, as if he were looking inward at something she couldn't see. "We'll always love her, Bree. No one can take her place."

"No one," she agreed.

"All our lives we'll remember how much we loved her. But if God wills, we can have children of our own someday. And we can love them with all the love Charity stirred in our hearts."

Bree flashed a bittersweet smile. "Yes, I want that. Children to love. Children of our own. And we'll tell them about Charity and how she brought us together and taught us so much about love. Imagine. Our children." Just the thought made her heart sing.

"Mr. Wingate...Miss Rowlands?"

They both jumped, startled, and looked toward the door, where Dr. Moreno stood in his surgical scrubs, a profound weariness in his eyes. As they scrambled to their feet he announced in his deep, distinctive voice, "We're done. Charity is in Recovery. You'll be able to see her soon."

"How is she?" cried Bree, crossing the room to the physician. "What did you find?"

"Ah, one question at a time. As I told the Dillards, she is doing quite well. You can see her in an hour or two."

"Then, she's going to be okay?" said Eric.

"Yes, in time. She's facing a difficult road for a while, but with proper care and attention, I don't think any of the obstacles will be insurmountable."

Brianna shook her head, puzzled. "What obstacles? I don't understand. Didn't the surgery correct the problem?"

"Yes, the immediate problem, Miss Rowlands, but you see—"

Eric broke in. "Dr. Moreno, exactly what's wrong with Charity?"

"Let's sit down, and I'll explain." They took the nearest chairs, Dr. Moreno facing Bree and Eric. "Charity has a congenital malposition of the stomach." He held out his hand, palm up, fingers curved. "Your stomach—a normal one—sits like a cup. Like this. Horizontal. But Charity's stomach is vertical. Some of the organs are pushing it out of place. It's as if a cord or tendon is wrapped around the stomach. That's what caused the violent episodes of vomiting."

"But you fixed it in surgery, right?" said Bree.

"Yes. We were able to reposition the stomach. We also patched a herniated area in the stomach opening. Eventually she'll be as good as new."

"How soon can Charity go home?" asked Bree. "To the Dillards, I mean."

"A few days, depending on how quickly we get her hydrated and she regains her strength. Charity will have a feeding tube in her side for several months while her stomach heals. I explained to the Dillards that she will require a great deal of tender loving care. I gave them some literature to instruct them in how to care for her in the days ahead."

"I hope they do a good job." Bree's throat constricted with a pang of regret. She should be the one taking Charity home and nursing her back to health. How could she be sure the Dillards would give her the careful attention she needed?

Eric held out his hand to Dr. Moreno. "Thank you for all your good work. We appreciate it."

"I'm glad it was something we could repair. We're all relieved. The little girl should have a good, long life ahead of her. You can see her in about an hour in the intensive care nursery. She'll be sleeping and won't know you're there, of course. And her arms and legs will be restrained. Don't let it frighten you. It's routine procedure after surgery."

Bree blinked back gathering tears. Tears of relief, gratitude and yearning. "Thank you, Doctor, for all you've done. I can't wait to see her."

But an hour later, when Bree and Eric made their way to the critical care nursery, they found Sam and Wanda Dillard already inside, hovering over Charity's bed. The homespun scene struck daggers in Brianna's heart, reminding her that Sam and Wanda were Charity's family now. They would be the ones taking her home, caring for her, watching her recover.

Bree gripped Eric's arm. "Let's go."

"Go? Don't you want to see Charity?"

"They only allow two in at a time. Who knows how long they'll be?"

"But we've waited all night. Another few minutes can't matter."

Tears broke in Brianna's eyes. "I can't stand to see her now, Eric. Not with the Dillards here. Knowing I can't have her. Can't take her home. Can't keep her for my little girl."

"I know how hard it is, Bree. I'm sorry. We've made a mess of things, haven't we. Letting Charity go too soon. Without a fight."

"I can't talk about it anymore, Eric. I just want to go back to my house and shower and change."

"Okay. Let's go. We can come back after breakfast."

On the way home Eric glanced over at Bree and said, "So what about us? Where do we stand?"

She gazed out the window at the pastel filigrees of dawn stretching across the horizon like pink satin ribbons. It was a new day. God promised His children a fresh supply of grace each morning. His unmerited favor. How Bree needed His mercy and compassion now, when her heart ached and all her emotions were raw, jumbled and confused. She loved Eric. And now, incredibly, he loved her, too! But could they really be a family without Charity? Would he be a constant reminder of what she had lost?

As Eric pulled into her driveway, he asked, "Do you want me to wait for you?"

She opened the car door and stepped outside, the brisk morning air filling her nostrils with the tang of salt spray. "No, don't wait, Eric. Go home. I know you want to shower and change, too." What she didn't add was that she needed some private time with God before she could agree to accept his ring.

He sounded worried, disappointed. "Suit yourself, Bree. I'll be back soon."

She waited until his car disappeared down the driveway, then slipped inside the silent, shadowed house and stole up to her room. Her father and sister were still asleep, and she didn't want to wake them. They would bombard her with questions she was simply too exhausted—and bewildered—to answer.

How long ago had she prayed and believed she had surrendered everything to God—her cares and heartaches, her dreams and desires? All to Jesus. He was all she needed, all she would ever need. His grace was sufficient.

But now this crisis with Charity. And Eric's startling proclamation of love. And this fresh spurt of grief over losing Charity. When would it end, this constant onslaught of problems and painful choices? Why couldn't yesterday's spiritual victories carry over to today? Why was she still desperately clutching what she had already given to God?

"It's not a once and for all thing, is it, Lord?" she said aloud as she settled in her favorite chair by the window. *"Oh, I know my salvation is a once and for all decision. But after that it's a moment by moment process, and I'm not handling it very well. I'm faced with a hundred big and little choices every day, and each time I must choose whether to trust You and take You at Your Word. Or will I muddle through again on my own strength?"*

As she gazed out at the ripe half melon of sun smudging away the darkness, she whispered, *"Help me, Lord. Let every breath I take and every beat of my heart be for You, Heavenly Father. No matter what happens, let me find my joy in You."*

Two weeks later the Rowlands clan threw a party to end all parties—a double engagement celebration for Andrew and Juliana, and Eric and Brianna. The house overflowed with laughing, chatting, exuberant party guests. They swarmed into the parlor with its streamers and balloons; they thronged the dining room with its bountiful spread of sandwiches, fondues, fruits and cheeses, chips and dips, and fancy confections. They spilled out into the backyard with its colorful Chinese lanterns, candlelit tables, and a live band playing romantic ballads.

"This time the party's official," Bree's father

boomed when he encountered her at the punch bowl. He looked as handsome as she had ever seen him, in his black tux, his eyes sparkling, a huge smile lighting his tanned, winsome face. "The whole world knows there's going to be a double wedding!"

Bree gave her father a warm bear hug. She didn't care if she wrinkled her new black velour dress with its shirred shoulder straps and flaring skirt. "I'm so happy for you, Daddy. You and Juliana make such a darling couple. She loves you so much."

"Not nearly as much as I love her." Her father's smile turned to a question as he cupped her face in his hands. "And how about you, my lovely daughter? Are you as happy as I am?"

She blinked rapidly. "Of course, Daddy. You know how much I love Eric. He's the only man I'll ever love."

"But I sense a wistfulness about you in the midst of all this revelry and merrymaking."

"You know what it is, Daddy. I still can't help thinking about Charity."

"Well, the way I hear it, Eric invited the Dillards and Charity to our party. So you'll get to see her again."

"Oh, Daddy, no! I don't think I could handle that—not at my engagement party!"

"I'm sorry, honey. You'd better talk to Eric about it."

She turned, her eyes searching the crowd for her fiancé. How could Eric have invited the Dillards when he knew how upset she would be to see Charity again? Where was his sensitivity, his consideration of her feelings? Didn't he know her better than that?

She wound her way through the crowd, her heart pounding with a sense of urgency. Where was Eric?

Maybe if he called the Dillards and explained the situation…

But no, it was too late. Bree stopped dead in her tracks. There were the Dillards in the foyer. They had just arrived, and Eric was greeting them. Oh, and now he was bringing them this way—Wanda, Pete and Sam with sweet little Charity in his arms.

Brianna's first impulse was to avoid this encounter at any cost. Being close to Charity again would lacerate all the emotional wounds that were just beginning to heal.

But it was too late. Sam came striding toward Bree, bouncing a smiling, bright-eyed Charity in his arms. She looked like a cherub in her ruffled pink dress, white tights and lacy booties. With a pink bow gracing her flaxen curls, she was irresistible. Bree's heart melted like warm wax, as Sam placed the cooing, rosy-cheeked baby in her arms.

A shy, abashed smile played on Sam's lips. "She's missed you, Miss Rowlands."

Bree squeezed Charity until she winced. "Oh, and I've missed her, too!" *Oh, Lord, help me! She feels so good in my arms. How can I let her go?*

"Did Mr. Wingate tell you our plans, Miss Rowlands?" Sam shifted from one foot to the other. In a suit a trifle too large, he obviously would have been more comfortable in sneakers and jeans.

"What plan?"

Eric stepped forward and took Bree's arm. "Maybe we should have this discussion where there's some privacy."

She gave him a searching glance. What was this all about? Was she about to hear more bad news? Were the Dillards moving to some distant state and taking Charity away forever?

"We can talk in my father's study down the hall," she said, her misgivings growing.

Eric turned and said something to Wanda, and moments later they had all gathered around her father's desk in his comfortable study. "Is something wrong?" Bree asked, still cuddling the baby in her arms. "Charity isn't having more problems, is she?"

"Oh, no, she's doing real well," said Wanda. "She's still on the feeding tube for another month or two, but the doctor says she's coming along fine."

Bree expelled a breath of relief. "Good. I was worried."

Eric, in her father's chair, turned to face her. "Bree, the reason we've gathered like this, Sam came to my office a few days ago. He wants to transfer to a school up north that specializes in his field of study."

Bree's heart sank. She had seen it coming. "You're going away?"

"To finish my last two years of college," said Sam. "If I take a full load and don't blow my grades, I'll graduate in two years."

Bree could hardly find her voice. "What about Charity?"

Sam seemed almost blasé. "Oh, I'm not taking her with me."

The mystery deepened. "Your mother's keeping her?"

"Oh, no, not me," said Wanda. "Charity's Sam's baby. This is his decision."

Bree glanced from face to face. "What decision? What are we talking about?"

Sam sat forward. There was something sweet and

heartrending in his eager, earnest expression and riotous Harpo Marx curls. "The thing is, Miss Rowlands, taking care of a baby is a lot harder than I figured. Especially now, with Charity's feeding tube and the doctor visits and all. I mean, I love my little girl to death, and I'll always be her daddy. No mistake about that. But like I told Mr. Wingate when I saw him the other day, I can't raise Charity the way a full-time mom and dad could. I've still got college and dating and working part time and carving out a future for myself."

Bree felt hope begin to rise like a seed planted by the water. "What are you saying, Sam?"

"I'm saying I want you and Mr. Wingate to raise Charity. When I heard the two of you were getting married, it just seemed right. She loves you both a whole bunch."

Brianna buried her face in Charity's downy hair so that no one could see her tears. *"Thank You, God!"* she whispered.

"So what do you say, Bree?" Eric's voice held a jubilant lilt. "Do we accept Sam's offer?"

She gazed at Sam through streaming tears. "Yes, yes, a thousand times, yes!"

Charity gazed up at Bree with her happy blue eyes and chortled, as if to echo her response, while one chubby fist gripped a strand of Bree's long hair.

"Hey, look," said Sam. "She's staking her own claim on you, Miss Rowlands. She wants you to be her mommy, and she's not about to let you go."

Bree hugged Charity to her breast and nuzzled her silky head. "And I'll never let go of her, either."

"There are some legal details to be worked out," said Eric, lapsing into his professional tone. "Sam still wants to be part of Charity's life. He wants limited visitation rights, and he wants Charity to grow up knowing he's her father.''

Bree nodded eagerly. ''Yes, we can do that, can't we, Eric?''

''Absolutely.''

''I have Charity's stuff out in the car,'' said Sam, standing and smoothing out his suit jacket. ''Should I bring it in now or wait till after the party?''

Bree's mind was still whirling with wonder. ''Uh, why don't you wait until after the party, Sam. We have lots of time.''

Wanda, her eyes misting with pride, joined her son and tucked her arm in his. ''Speaking of time, Sam, maybe it's time for us to join the rest of the guests and give Charity some time alone with her new parents.''

''Sure, Mom. Just give me a minute.'' Sam ambled over to Bree and awkwardly scooped Charity up in his arms. He kissed each round cheek and the tip of her button nose. ''You be a good girl, Charity. And don't forget your daddy, okay? I'll come see you soon.'' With a little choking sound, he handed Charity back to Brianna. ''Take care of her, Miss Rowlands. She's a keeper, that's for sure.'' His voice cracked and a muscle twitched by his mouth. ''Maybe you can send me some pictures and videos, so I can see her walking and talking and stuff like that.''

Bree wrapped her arms around Sam and Charity. ''I will. Every month. I promise.''

After the Dillards left, Eric gathered Brianna and Charity into his arms and kissed them both, Bree on her lips in a long, lingering kiss and Charity lightly on the cheek. ''We have our family, Bree,'' he whispered as he nuzzled her ear. ''A loving family, a love-filled marriage and a loving God to watch over us always.''

She brushed a happy tear from her lashes. "Can't ask for more than that, can we."

Eric hoisted Charity up and swung her high, then circled Bree's waist with his free arm. "So let's go join our party guests and share our good news. My darling, it's high time we celebrated!"

Epilogue

❦

Brianna couldn't see Sam. He was up on stage in line to receive his diploma, but a thousand people in the stadium blocked her view. "I can't see him, Eric," she lamented. "And I so wanted Charity to see her daddy graduate."

"Here, let me." Eric lifted the fidgety three-year-old over his head and onto his shoulders. "There! Now she can see."

"Giddy up, horsie!" Charity bounced up and down, her pink taffeta dress rippling in the warm June breeze, her mop of golden curls bobbing with her. "Where's Daddy?" she crooned. "Where's my daddy?"

Bree pointed. "He's up there. See him, honey? Right there. Walking across the stage in his cap and gown. Look, he's smiling and waving to you. Waving his diploma. He did it, sweetheart, just like he said he would."

"That's our boy!" boomed Bree's father, so that everyone in the bleachers around them could hear.

"Andrew, control yourself," chided Juliana, beside him. "People are looking."

"Aw, come on, Jewel, darling, where's your feisty Italian bravado? Your usual extravagance and bombast? Where's that great voice of yours the whole world deserves to hear?"

"All right, Andrew. If you insist." Juliana stood up and tossed a plucky smile at Pete and Wanda Dillard. "This is for your son." She put her hands to her mouth, threw her shoulders back and shouted in her full-bodied soprano, "Hooray for Sam Dillard!"

"That's my girl!" said Andrew, laughing as heads three rows down turned back to look. "She's never at a loss for words."

When the last graduate had crossed the stage and the final strains of "Pomp and Circumstance" had faded in the balmy air, the Rowlands, the Wingates and the Dillards filed out of the stadium with a thousand other proud parents and relatives.

It wasn't a moment too soon for Bree. Three hours she had sat on that hard bench, and now she was in misery.

Eric slipped his arm around her. "You okay, honey?"

She smoothed out her full, princess-style dress. "I will be when I can sit down in a nice soft chair."

"Try to hold on a while longer." He looked around, still bouncing Charity on his shoulders. "Now, if we can just find Sam in this crowd."

"He said to meet him by the big oak tree by the student center," said Wanda.

"That's this way," said Pete, gesturing toward a sprawling white stucco building in the distance.

Juliana bent down and removed her three-inch heels.

"I hope no one minds if I walk in the grass in my stocking feet."

Andrew took her leather pumps and fell into step beside her. "I love a woman who's not afraid to go barefoot in public."

Eric tossed Brianna a sly smile. "Care to go barefoot, too?"

She gave him a cunning look. "What are you trying to do, Mr. Wingate? Keep me barefoot and pregnant?"

He patted her rounded tummy. "Well, one out of two isn't bad."

"Papa Eric," chimed Charity, "let me pat the baby, too!"

Eric stooped down and let Charity place her hand on what Brianna fondly called her watermelon figure.

Bree placed her hand over Charity's. "Feel the baby kicking, honey? He says he wants to come out and play with his big sister."

"That's me!" Charity thumped her chest with pride. "I'm bigger, and he's the baby."

"That's right, and he'll be coming to see you any day now." Eric held Charity in place as he straightened to his full height. Then he broke into a gallop, as she wound her arms around his neck and cried, "Giddap, horsie!"

Bree called after them, "If I try to keep up with you two, I'll have this baby today."

Eric dropped back beside her. "I meant it about kicking your shoes off. It might make it easier to walk in this uneven grass."

"No, I'm managing quite well in my two-inch pumps."

"I see him!" cried Wanda. "There's Sam, by the tree, just as he said."

They all hastened through the thinning crowd to the gnarled oak that cast shade over half the student center. Sam, still in his cap and gown, embraced his parents, gave Juliana a hug, shook hands with Andrew and Eric, and stared in amazement at Brianna's blossoming middle. "Man alive! Are you sure you shouldn't be at the hospital instead of my graduation?"

Bree smiled tolerantly. "I told the baby he had to wait another day or so. I wasn't about to miss your big day."

Sam bent over and brushed a kiss on Brianna's cheek. "Thanks. For everything. You've been great." Then he turned his attention to the little moppet on Eric's shoulders. He held out his hands and said, "Where's my little girl?"

Charity held out her hands, too. "Here I am, Daddy!"

Sam dislodged his daughter from Eric's shoulders and swung her up in the air. "Did you see me up there, Charity? I made it, honey! I did it for you!" He removed his washboard cap and placed it on Charity's head, tilting it so it wouldn't cover her eyes. He flicked the tassel, and his own eyes misted over as he touched his daughter's plump cheek. "Someday you'll have one of these caps, too, pretty girl. We'll all be watching you cross the stage for your diploma. And won't I be proud of my little girl!"

"But no more graduations for a while," said Juliana. "Everybody is growing up too fast!"

"Let's head for our cars," Bree's father trumpeted. "We have a rousing party and plenty of guests waiting for us at home. And I want to get out the bibs and devour some of those fancy shrimp tidbits before they're gone."

Eric stayed back with Brianna, as everyone else surged ahead. He wound his arm around her shoulder and pulled her against him so they could walk in sync, as one. It was the end of a perfect day. Beyond the spiky fronds of palm trees, a blood-red sun was already hugging the horizon while sweeping strokes of blue brushed the sky. The blazing sunset framed a perfect silhouette of lanky Sam Dillard in his flowing robe, trotting across the wide expanse of lawn with his lovely, laughing daughter riding his shoulders.

"Looks like Charity's in her glory," Eric noted, "with so many people around to love her."

"And soon there'll be another," said Bree in a light, lyrical voice. "Another darling baby to love."

Eric chuckled. "But with Charity, I expect more sibling rivalry than sisterly love for the first few years."

Bree rested her head on Eric's broad shoulder. "That's all right, sweetheart. We have enough love for both of them."

Eric kissed the top of Bree's windblown hair. "You can say that again, my beauty. Between the two of us, we have enough love to last a thousand lifetimes."

* * * * *

Dear Reader,

I hope you're enjoying the continuing saga of Reverend Andrew Rowlands and his three spirited daughters. I know I've enjoyed making the Reverend the kind of devoted, fun-loving, larger-than-life daddy we gals dream of. And yet Andrew is human just like the rest of us. Even as he ministers to others, he struggles with heavy issues in his own life—problems that lead him to search for a closer walk with his Heavenly Father.

Andrew's three daughters must confront their own complex issues, as well. This time, it's Brianna's turn. She faces a series of losses that threaten to overwhelm her. But each time she realizes afresh that God is there for her. Both Brianna and Reverend Rowlands come to know Christ better as they experience a roller-coaster ride of conflicting crises and emotions. They are reminded that Jesus loves them with perfect love… and perfect love casts out fear.

It's a lesson for all of us to remember. When we look outward at our troubling circumstances, we may experience fear and anxiety. When we look inward at ourselves, we often feel inadequate. Only as we keep our eyes on Jesus can we experience His comforting presence and face life with confidence and joy. Trust Him, and He will fill you with His love, joy and peace!

I'd love to hear from you, my friend. Write me c/o Steeple Hill Books, 300 East 42nd Street, New York, New York 10017. And please keep reading! May God bless you with His very best!

Carole Gift Page

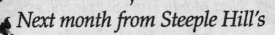

Next Month From Steeple Hill's

Love Inspired®

BLESSED BABY
by *Lois Richer*

Book #3 of
IF WISHES WERE WEDDINGS

Briony Green has given up hope of having her own family—until she is sent a miracle from heaven above. After her twin sister dies, a grieving Briony is shocked to discover her sister had given birth to a child, which had been given up for adoption. Determined to lavish her niece with love, Briony arrives at the home of Tyrell Demens, who is in way over his head caring for the active toddler. Sparks fly between the secretly tormented widower and the feisty Briony as they join forces to nurture the blessed baby girl. Now it's only a matter of time before they acknowledge that they are meant to be a family!

Don't miss
BLESSED BABY
On sale October 2001

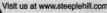